EAT

PAUL MANNERING

SEVERED PRESS
HOBART TASMANIA

EAT

WWW.SEVEREDPRESS.COM

ISBN: 978-1-925597-06-6

CHAPTER 1

Duty officer Naota Mitsuro focused on the console in front of him. The sky through the wide Perspex windshield of the Japanese freighter, *Sapporo Sunrise*, was dark and filled with the ice of a stormy spring night on the North Pacific Ocean. The green glow of the radar and other sensors were his only view of what might lie ahead.

Satisfied that the seas around them were clear in all directions, Mitsuro opened the side door and stepped out onto the icy steel walkway. With gloved hands cupped around the end of his cigarette, he lit up and took a deep drag.

The shrieking northerly wind tore at his face like frozen fingernails. He smoked quickly, one eye on the dull warning lights of the console inside. From here, Mitsuro could hear the twang and creak of the steel ropes that connected the *Sapporo* to the ship they towed. The *Mikhail Lazarov*, a Russian-made cruise liner, one of the small ones that only took a hundred passengers. After going unpaid for three months, the *Mikhail's* crew had deserted in the port of Vancouver. Now she was on her way to Japan, destined for the scrap yards.

A new sound rose above the wind, a rumbling, like a thunderstorm, that went on and grew louder. Mitsuro's first thought was an earthquake; the deep bass vibration of a seismic event had a similar sound. Then he heard the hiss of water spraying from a cresting wave and dropped his cigarette.

Akutōnami!

Throwing the bridge door open, Mitsuro dashed to the control console and hit the general alarm. The bow of the 600-foot long ship dipped, and the vessel bore down into a void while the rising wall of a rogue wave came rushing towards them.

The ship's officer secured himself and began to pray as the klaxon of the alarm was drowned out by the roaring mountain of seawater that now filled his view.

Her engines howling, the *Sapporo* powered up the slope of the oncoming wave and then, the tempest erupted. White-foam exploded over the bow of the ship, sweeping the forward deck clear and flooding over the bridge. The ship foundered under the crushing weight. The crew scrambling from their bunks and stations below decks crashed to the floor with the force of the impact.

With the buoyancy of the 10,000-ton ship forcing her upwards, the *Sapporo* tore through the wave and resurfaced, millions of gallons of seawater pouring off her deck and hull.

The ship's captain, Takahiro Fujiwara, stumbled onto the bridge, demanding that Mitsuro explain. The deck officer picked himself up from the floor, struggling to stand up straight as water poured out of the bridge through the open side door.

"*Akutōnami!* Rogue wave!" Mitsuro shouted.

Fujiwara had been a sailor all his life; he knew they were lucky to have survived their encounter with the random ship killers that surged across the seas for no apparent reason.

Snatching up a radio handset, he barked instructions to his

crew. All hands check and report any damage. A team was ordered to activate the bilge pumps to clear any flooding.

"Mitsuro! Check the tow-lines."

The officer bowed with a bob of his head and scuttled off the bridge. His boots clanged on the metal walkway as he ran down to the stern of the ship. Here, steel cables, bound together to form a rope as thick as the sailor's wrist, ran out into the darkness where the derelict ship they were towing floated.

Instead of a taut, creaking line, the cable lay on the deck, limp as a caught squid. The rope trailed off the end of the ship and into the cold ocean.

Mitsuro took a heavy flashlight from a steel cabinet. The 5000 lumens beam turned night into day for a range of nearly a mile. The churning sea behind the *Sapporo* was empty. The *Mikhail Lazarov* was gone.

CHAPTER 2

Dale woke to the shuddering vibration of an impact on the hull of the *Crystal Blue*. One berth aft, he heard the muffled cursing of Keith, owner and self-proclaimed skipper of the 60-foot yacht, as he tumbled out of bed.

With a tired sigh, Dale slid out of bed and put his feet into two inches of seawater on the cabin floor.

"Fuck," he yelped. "Shona! Wake up! We're taking on water!"

He didn't wait to see if the woman sleeping next to him had registered his alarm. Instead, Dale pulled on a T-shirt and headed topside.

The sun was breaking the horizon, casting an eerie glow across the ocean. Lily, retirement age and loving it, had the wheel, her face grim as she squinted into the distance.

"What the fuck did we hit?" Dale asked.

"I don't know." Lily gripped the wheel with white knuckles. "Logan's up front. You might ask him."

Dale ran up the narrow deck, the swinging sails blocking his view. "Logan?"

"Over here, mate," Logan replied. Old enough to be Dale's

dad, he and Lily had come on board in Sydney, Australia. Now he lay face down, head and chest hanging over the bow of the yacht. "I think we're holed," Logan announced as Dale crouched down beside him.

"Bad?"

Logan raised his head and nodded. "Possibly. It's likely to be debris from the Japanese tsunami, back in 2011."

"What did we hit?" Dale scanned the calm ocean around them.

"Telegraph pole? Shipping container? Who knows?"

"We're taking on water," Dale announced. "If we can't patch it…"

"Yes, I hear you. Perhaps I should get the women onto the life raft. Just in case, eh?"

Dale nodded, standing up and hurrying back down the deck.

Keith stood in the hatchway in shorts and a Hawaiian shirt. "We're taking on water!" the older man bellowed.

"Yes, Keith. We hit some Japanese tsunami debris. I'm going below to see if I can patch the hole. I think you should get everyone on to the life raft just as a precaution."

Keith bristled. "Bloody Japanese! I'll sue the mongrels."

"Sure," Dale nodded. "But right now, could you get out of my way?"

Keith climbed out onto the deck. Dale slipped past him and climbed down.

"Shona?"

"I'm here." She sounded calm and that helped Dale's nerves. She stepped out of the tiny cabin they shared, shorts, sneakers, and a lightweight jacket zipped up, ready for action as she was tying her long hair back.

"We're taking on water," Dale stated the obvious as it sloshed around their ankles.

"Can we patch it?" Both Shona and Dale had been raised on sailboats, and of the six people on board, they were the only ones with the experience and qualifications to run a sail yacht.

"I hope so. Get Mrs. Tulley and all the supplies you can. Prep the life raft. Just in case."

Shona shot him a concerned look. "Just in case," she echoed and grabbed a small knapsack.

Dale hurried through the narrow corridor and lifted the trapdoor that led to the narrow space between the hull and the cabins. Dark water boiled up through the doorway. "Shit."

"Dale? Is everything okay?" Elizabeth Tulley, Keith's young wife, was about as much use on a boat like this as a brass band on a submarine.

"Everything's fine, Mrs. Tulley. Get your life-jacket on and go up on deck, okay?"

"Oh…okay." She was wearing a floral-patterned sundress and, if she was true to form, a scandalously small bikini underneath.

Dale often wondered if Elizabeth's way of coping with being dragged on a yacht voyage across the Pacific, from Australia to Japan, via Hawaii was to stay stoned on prescription drugs. Though if he was married to an arrogant prick like Keith Tulley, he would probably want to be wasted all the time too.

The water surged again. Dale took a deep breath and reached through the trapdoor as far as he could and groped for any sign of a tear in the outer hull. Cold water swirled past his hand and he felt the jagged edges of a ragged hole in the aluminum shell.

Pulling back, Dale raised his head above water. It was deep

enough now that he could barely touch the underside of the trapdoor without ducking his head under. In the gloom, a dark lump popped up out of the water. Dale blinked and then leapt up with a yell as a massive rat lunged at him.

The rodent dog-paddled for the light of the entrance, and Dale shivered as he watched it go. He hated rats. Their cold tails, sharp teeth, and general squirminess.

Shona came down the ladder to the water's edge. "Dale?"

"I'm here!" He stood up, the water now around his waist.

"She's done, get out of there!" Shona yelled.

Dale waded down the narrow corridor, snatching up things that floated past. By the time he reached the ladder going up to the hatch, he had an armload of torches, dried food, and an extra first-aid kit. "Here, take this lot." He pushed his loot at Shona who gathered it up.

"Come on," she insisted.

"I'll be right up." Dale turned and plunged into the water again. Half-swimming, half-wading, he pulled himself into the tiny cabin he shared with Shona.

The batteries that gave the yacht its internal power supply shorted out and Dale was plunged into darkness. Feeling his way, he found the belt with his dive knife and the slack rubber sling of his spear gun, both hanging from the hook where he had left them. There was now less than a foot of air between the water and the ceiling. Dale pushed himself off the wall and out into the corridor. The yacht groaned and rolled off center. The weight of the water threatened to capsize the boat, and the sudden change in position threw Dale against the wall.

"Dale!" Shona screamed. He tried to reply, calling out that he was fine, but he couldn't get enough air to shout. A stabbing pain burst through his chest as he inhaled. The sharp salt taste of the water swirled through his mouth. Choking and coughing, Dale swam up, nearly stunning himself on the low ceiling of the narrow corridor.

Rolling onto his back, he breathed with a sharp whine. The pain in his ribs became excruciating. Kicking weakly, he swam backwards, the last of the air vanishing under the rising water as his head bumped against the ladder.

Hands grabbed Dale under the arms and yanked upwards. He took a deep breath as he slid out onto the deck. Logan and Shona were watching him anxiously.

"Go... " Dale muttered. "She's going down."

"You're lucky, mate," Logan said with his usual dry wit. "Another couple of minutes and we would have left without you."

Together, Shona and Logan helped Dale to his feet; he hissed at the pain and let them half-carry him across the pitching deck.

"Jump!" Shona shouted. Logan hesitated.

"Go on, mate," Dale said. "We're right behind you."

Logan let go of Dale and leapt into the water. The yellow vest life jacket he wore brought him bobbing to the surface a moment later. He swam towards the black-and-orange octagon of the life-raft that floated a few feet away.

"Can you make it?" Shona's face was etched with worry.

"Sure I can." Dale tried to smile and just looked crazed.

The yacht deck rolled underneath them and they both jumped. The mast slammed down into the water with a thunderous cracking sound. Dale came up, gasping in shock and pain. Shona was already on the surface. She grabbed Dale by the hand and drew him closer, the buoyancy of her life jacket keeping them both up.

Kicking strongly, Shona dragged Dale to the life raft. Hands reached out and dragged them into the boat. Spots danced in Dale's eyes and his vision blurred.

"Motherfuu…" he managed before passing out.

CHAPTER 3

Dale became aware of voices. Logan was reciting a list. "One signaling torch, one repair kit, one whistle, one sea anchor, and two first-aid kits."

"Twelve days food and water for six people. We can stretch that to eighteen days if we are careful," Shona said. He could feel the vibration of her voice through the back of his skull. He must be lying with his head in her lap.

"What if Dale doesn't make it?" That was Keith. Dale tried to tell his employer he was a bastard, but ended up groaning instead.

"Dale?" a damp cloth wiped his forehead. He opened his eyes and saw Shona's blonde hair hanging down over his face.

"Hey, babe…" he whispered. She smiled and kissed him.

"Careful now," Logan warned. "He took quite a blow to the ribs. Let's not make it worse."

"I'm okay. Is everyone okay?" Dale tried to sit up, wincing at the pain. He looked around and saw Keith, Logan, Lily, Elizabeth, and Shona, all present and correct. Elizabeth looked wet and dazed; the rest looked wet and frightened.

"So now what the hell do we do?" Keith did not like being

out of control. It made him petulant and irritating.

"We keep calm and rest," Dale said. "It's important we conserve our energy."

Logan nodded, his expression deep in thought.

"Does this thing have a motor?" Keith looked around the inflatable rubber boat. The tent-like canopy overhead meant there was barely room to stand as they rose and fell on the gentle swell.

"No motor. It does have some paddles. But, like I said, it is better to rest." Dale kept his voice calm and reasonable. He wanted nothing more than to scream and yell.

"The canopy, acts like a sail, it will take us where the wind blows. There's ocean currents though, so they'll take us west, towards the Philippines." Shona spoke with a calm authority. Dale wanted to kiss her again. She got it.

"So how long till that happens?" Keith expected answers. He talked to everyone as if he was chairing a meeting at his corporate office in Sydney.

"Maybe a week?" Shona suggested.

"Our last logged position on the GPS, put us forty nautical miles north-east of Nauru," Dale explained. "So, if the wind doesn't blow, that puts us in the middle of the equatorial currents. They flow east. Two weeks, maximum. We'll either hit civilization, or stray into commercial shipping routes. We have flares, and any ship that sees them, will investigate."

"It's a big ocean, what if we don't see any ships?" Keith asked.

"Keith, with all due respect, the eastern side of the Pacific Ocean is like a freeway. There are so many ships going back and forth, we won't have to take the first one that sees us. We can tell them we'll wait for a nice cruise-liner, something with a decent bar and a buffet."

Keith frowned; Dale knew that the tycoon had no sense of humor and the young sailor was pushing it. The tension broke like overstretched bubblegum when Elizabeth let out a barking laugh.

"Look! Dolphins!" She was pointing out to sea. Everyone crawled over to peer out through the gap in the canopy. The water broke with the spray of a pod of bottlenose dolphins exhaling.

"Dolphins are your favorite, aren't they, darlin'?" Keith seemed gruffly affectionate towards his wife. She was at least thirty years his junior, a cosmetically enhanced and vapid redhead with freckles that were probably cute when she was little. Dale and Shona had giggled that the difference in the Tulleys' IQ scores was probably the same as their age difference.

While Elizabeth cooed and clapped at the dolphins, Logan crawled over to where Dale lay propped up against the soft inflatable wall of the boat.

"Let's strap that rib of yours," he said. "It won't help with the healing process, but it might make you more comfortable."

"We were lucky to have a doctor on the boat," Dale said. Shona squeezed his hand.

"Semi-retired, remember. I mostly do locum work now. More time to spend with my girl." Logan turned his head and smiled at Lily. She beamed back at him, as calm and elegant in the current crisis as she was on the day she caught a thirty-pound tuna over the rail of the *Crystal Blue*.

Dale tried to breathe steadily as Logan wrapped a gauze bandage around his ribs. It did help; the feeling of consistent pressure was somehow comforting.

By the end of the first day, they stopped talking to each

other. Logan and Shona dished out food and water at dusk. Dale scanned the horizon, looking for any sign of a ship, or land. Elizabeth was quiet for the first night; by morning, she had come off whatever pills she was on and slipped into a depressed state. Crying and slapping at anyone who tried to comfort her, she curled up on a towel and refused to eat.

It was easiest to slip over the side to use the bathroom; no one commented on it. Their living quarters had been cramped before, but this was extreme.

Shona knelt next to Dale, the spear gun with a meter-long aluminum shaft on the stretched band, ready to fire. She watched the water, looking for any sign of a fish. So far, she'd only seen seaweed and gyre debris.

"Remember that restaurant in Fiji? Right on the beach," Dale said, his gaze never leaving the horizon.

"The one where they'd clean and cook your catch after a day's fishing?" Shona grinned at the memory. "They cooked a great steak if I recall correctly."

Dale flushed at the memory. "Only that first night," he reminded her.

"Yeah, the fish *I* caught on the second day, they were delish."

Moments like this were all rare in the interminable hours of waiting. They all slept more, conserving energy, passing time. Dale insisted that someone keep watch while the others slept, the loaded flare gun close at hand.

After two days, Elizabeth started to crawl around the life raft. She moaned and muttered. Complaining of cramps, headaches, and needing her meds. She asked Keith constantly to go to the pharmacy and get her prescriptions filled. By nightfall on the third day, Keith had run out of patience. When Elizabeth asked him again to get her script filled, he hit her. Not an open-handed slap, but a punch in the face with a clenched fist. His hands were large, with knuckles that stood out like blunt spikes. The crack of the impact rolled out across the waves.

"Jesus!" Dale shouted.

"Keith, that wasn't necessary!" Logan scolded.

Keith turned on them. "I had to shut the fucking bitch up!"

Shona and Lily dragged Elizabeth over to the other side of the life raft. She was whimpering, and her right eye was already swelling closed.

"We have to keep it together," Logan insisted. "I know it is hard, we're all tired and stressed. But she's clearly going through some kind of withdrawal."

"Withdrawal?" Keith's face darkened. "My wife is not a fucking junkie!"

"Of course she's not." Dale raised his hands. "She's just not feeling well. Logan? Is there anything in the first-aid kit we can give her?"

"Maybe some pain-killers. Codeine that is. It should help her sleep at least."

"You got any Scotch in there?" Keith's forced jocularity fell flat.

Elizabeth took two tablets and swallowed half her ration of water. Lily cradled the other woman's head in her lap and stroked her hair. "You know my mother always said that freckles were angel's kisses," she said as the younger woman's other eye closed and she settled into a doze.

Silence fell over the boat. They sat, their legs to the center, backs leaning against the soft walls. Lily nodded off, her hands curled in Elizabeth's hair. Shona snuggled up against Dale and he held her, trying to ignore the growing ache in his balls. Even on the Crystal Blue, there had been enough privacy in the cabins for lovemaking. Keith took the watch position, twisted away from everyone else and staring out over the sparkling water. Logan had found a Bible in the supplies and passed the time by reading it silently, occasionally shaking his head as if in disbelief or disagreement.

It was still dark when Dale woke up. He blinked, trying to make out what was happening.

"Fucking prick!" he heard Elizabeth snarl.

"Sit down, you dumb bitch," Keith snapped back.

Dale sat up. "Guys?"

"I fucking told you. You ever hit me again, I would fucking kill you!" Elizabeth's voice rose to a shriek, drowning out the voices of the others calling for calm.

Elizabeth was kneeling spread-legged on the soft floor of the life raft, a savage expression on her face. She held the spear gun, aimed at Keith, the moonlight glinting off the aluminum barbs at the bolt's head.

"You stupid cunt," Keith sneered. He sat with his arms wide, the flare gun gripped in his right hand, calling her bluff.

Elizabeth screamed, her hand clenched, and the spear gun fired with a dull *THWACK*. The end of the spear jutted two inches out of Keith's upper thigh. He screamed, jerking against the sudden agony. The flare gun exploded, the flammable charge inside it careening across the life raft and exploding at the deep seam between the floor and the inflated wall.

Thick red smoke filled the space under the canopy. Between the screams and coughing, Dale lunged for the bailing scoop. He started hurling water into the boat. "Perchlorate!" Logan yelled. "We need to smother it!" He snatched up the sodden towel and plunged it into the fizzing hole in the boat. "Shit!" he howled as his arms vanished underwater up to the elbows.

The flare bobbed to the surface a couple of meters away from the boat. The smoke started to clear, revealing they had a new problem. One of the eight sides of the inflatable raft had deflated. At floor-level, a hole had burned through a square foot of the rubber skin, letting the seawater flush into the boat.

"Logan, get the patch kit!" Dale had reversed his bailing, and now tried to empty the life raft.

The doctor didn't respond. Dale looked through the red fog and saw the older man being tended to by Lily. One of his hands was red and blistered. Lily was bandaging his wounded arm, and Logan's eyes were screwed shut against the agony of saltwater on the raw wound.

"Everyone, to the other side, keep the hole above the water!" Shona grabbed Elizabeth and dragged her backwards. Lily shuffled back, Logan following her, holding his arm up and staring as if his hand had become demonically possessed.

"Keith! Move!" Dale looked at his boss. Keith had gone pale. The blood had drained out of his face and was now mixing with the seawater Dale was bailing.

"Oh shit." Dale dropped the scoop and rolled Keith onto his side. The long shaft of the spear had gone right through the thick meat of his thigh and punched a hole in the rubber boat's inflatable cell. As the spear ripped free, water and air hissed through the puncture and added to the wash sliding around inside.

Dale heaved Keith over to where the women had bunched up. The shift in weight tilted the floor and bloody-filled water flooded over them. Elizabeth screamed.

"Don't pull the spear out," Logan gasped. "He'll bleed to death. Put… Put a pressure bandage around the wound. Bind it tight."

Dale nodded, looking to Shona. She took a deep breath. "I can do it."

"I know." Dale smiled and pressed the second first-aid kit at her.

The floor of the rubber boat had tilted above the water on the damaged side. Dale grabbed the bailing scoop and started bucketing water out through the gap in the canopy. The thought of sharks weighed heavily on him. All the old legends about how they could smell a drop of blood in a cubic mile of water. He'd seen sharks, even dived with them. Sharks are harmless. If a shark comes near you, just bop it on the nose, and it will soon bugger off.

As he bailed, he watched the water outside. The swells were smooth and low, as they had been for the last week. After five minutes of constant bailing, the seawater was mostly gone from inside the boat. Dale's strength had gone with it. Every breath sent shards of pain stabbing through his chest.

Shona had bound a tight bandage around Keith's leg, but he was still out in a dead faint. Dale wondered how the fuck things had gotten so bad so fast.

CHAPTER 4

Dale lay in the stricken life raft, watching Keith's chest rise and fall. He was waiting for it to stop. In the four hours since Elizabeth shot him, Keith hadn't died.

Waiting for him to die, waiting for his chest to shudder and grind to a halt in its slow pistoning up and down, was hypnotic. Dale realized that he wished Keith would die.

On the yacht, Keith had been the boss, the man with the money. So Dale and Shona had taken his shit and smiled, absorbed the stupid demands and querulous abuse, all the time reminding themselves that he paid well to ensure that everyone had a great trip.

Not anymore though. They were off the clock and Keith was going to die. From blood loss or by drowning when Dale finally pushed his head under the water and held it there.

Something bumped against Dale's back. He moved slightly, getting comfortable. The bump came again, this time under his butt. Dale sat up, his hands pressed against the floor of the life raft. A shape pressed up against the floor, and slowly scraped under the boat. Dale watched it, then scrambled to the edge, looking to see if it might be a rock, perhaps they were nearing an island?

The sun was almost directly overhead and showed nothing but the gentle swell and sparkling water of the tropics. Dale knelt, leaning on the sagging side of the boat and studied the horizon. The first dorsal fin broke the water less than a foot away from him. The sleek grey body of the shark swept past and went under the boat again. Within a minute, there were others. Dale didn't know much about shark species beyond the obvious, but these were some big bastards.

He watched them circle, trying to count the number. Four? Maybe six. Dale felt sure the largest of them was a great white. Jaws material. Moving carefully, he found a flashlight and flicked it on. The beam swept over the floor of the raft. Blood was washing from the sodden bandage around Keith's leg and a thin trail of red was running out through the hole in the boat.

The others were asleep, so Dale carefully rolled a towel and made a barricade to stop more bloody water draining out into the ocean.

Laying the towel near the edge of the hole seemed like the best bet. With the flashlight rolling around on the floor, Dale positioned the towel carefully. The life raft jolted upwards, and Dale saw the flash of a wide mouth made entirely of triangular teeth. A primal terror gripped him and he couldn't even scream. Some reflex made him jerk backwards before he had even formed the conscious thought, *Shark! In the boat!*

The smooth, pointed head pushed up through the ragged hole the flare had made. The adhesive patch peeled back as the shark thrashed left and right, trying to get free. The violence of it woke everyone else up. Dale tried to ignore the screaming from behind him as he scrambled for the spear gun. They only had the one spear. It was still in Keith's thigh, the sharp end of it sticking three inches out of the back of his leg.

Dale jumped on Keith. The man groaned; his skin seemed hot and feverish. "Shona! Grab his fucking feet. I need to get the spear out!"

She did, and clambering over Lily and Elizabeth, Shona pressed her weight down on Keith's feet. Dale grabbed the blood-slicked aluminum shaft and pulled on it. Keith howled and fresh blood oozed from the wound. Dale tightened his grip and twisted the shaft. With a slow, wet sucking sound, the spear slid out the back of Keith's leg.

"Oh you fucking cunt!" Keith screamed, his body convulsing and thrashing in agony. "Fucking shit! Arse! Fucking cunnnggghhh!"

Dale ignored him; instead, he snatched the spear gun and slotted the bolt in place. Pulling the heavy rubber band back, he twisted around, ready to shoot the shark in the face. The killer fish was gone.

"My fucking leg…" Keith moaned. Shona re-tied the bandage as heavy drops of dark blood smeared on the lifeboat floor.

"Sharks. Fucking sharks…" Dale panted.

"We are safe in here, aren't we?" Lily spoke up for the first time in hours.

"Get me out of here, please!" Elizabeth was looking around in a panic. Everyone from Keith to Lily just stared at her with blank and tired expressions.

"Calm down, Mrs. Tulley," Dale said. "They've gone now. You're safe."

"Can we pack the hole with something?" Logan asked. Dale gave the older man credit. He must be in terrible pain with his burned hand. But he was keeping quiet, contained, and most importantly, calm.

"The bag of supplies," Shona suggested. "It's big enough."

They took a quick vote; Lily and Logan agreed with Shona and Dale. Keith and Elizabeth didn't vote.

Shona stripped everything out of the waterproof bag; all their food, water, and the first-aid kits. Everything was in its own, sealed plastic packaging. She pushed the contents to the safe end of the life raft and handed Dale the empty bag.

"Where's my knife?" he asked.

"I…" Shona looked around. "I thought it was in the bag?"

Dale searched the bag, "No. Guys, there's a knife? A decent-sized one? In a black sheath?" Logan and Lily shook their heads.

"No one's seen your fucking knife," Keith growled through gritted teeth. "Christ, Logan, can you give me something for the pain?"

"Give Keith two codeine tablets please, Lily." Logan hadn't taken anything for his burn. Dale could see the bandage around his hand starting to show a yellow seepage. The doctor was one tough old bird.

"Just a sip," Lily warned Keith as she poured a splash of water into a mug.

"Oh fuck off," Keith growled, taking the tablets and the cup.

The others watched him drink. Dale had insisted, and they all agreed to ration their food and water. Everyone had been confident on the first day they would be rescued within a week, if not sooner. Now, they watched as Keith tapped the bottom of the cup to get the last drop.

"Shonny, give me a hand." Dale flattened the bag out and pressed it against the ragged hole in the floor of the boat. "Don't suppose there's any duct tape in the kit?" he asked.

"Bloody useless," Keith muttered.

Dale took a deep breath, his fists clenched on the bag; Shona's hand was a cooling touch on his arm.

"It was worth a shot, Keith," Dale replied. They left the bag tucked into the bottom of the boat, covering the hole and maybe stopping the entire ocean from pushing up to join them.

They sat higher on the inflatable sides as water sloshed around their feet. The canopy meant they had to lean forward, and Dale felt the bruised muscles of his chest protest.

"You okay, babe?" Shona sat beside him, her arm slipping around his waist.

"Yeah." He gave her a smile. Together, there was nothing they couldn't survive.

"You win a cookie," she said and grinned. It was infectious and he grinned back. Shona distributed single-serve cookies to each of the survivors. Only Keith refused.

Dale tipped the last of his cookie crumbs into his mouth and kept an eye on the occasional dorsal fin that breached the surface as the sharks circled.

CHAPTER 5

Sleep was a challenge with their feet in the shallow water. Dale woke up from a doze, needing to piss. Extracting himself from Shona's embrace, he shushed her softly when she woke up with a start.

"I gotta pee," he whispered.

She shivered. "Yeah, me too."

Dale could feel his balls climbing up around his armpits at visions of a shark bursting out of the water and snapping his tackle off. He spared a thought for the girls and gave a silent sigh of relief as he urinated into the sea.

Turning back, he saw Shona clenching her thighs right behind him. "Hold my hand," she whispered. He took it, and she shucked her shorts and undies down with the other hand. With some wiggling, she got far enough over the side.

"A fucking shark is going to bite me on the bum," she whispered. Even in the twilight, he could see she was terrified.

"You'll be fine, just relax and pee."

After a moment, she wriggled forward, and Dale lifted her back onto the rubber deck. She crouched, pulling everything up, and then went back down to wash her hands in the swirling seawater.

Logan and Lily silently followed suit, he first, and then holding her securely as she worked her buttocks over the edge of the inflatable.

"Ooh!" Lily squealed. Everyone started in panic until she laughed; a clear and bright sound in the rising darkness. "A wave splashed me. It's cold."

Logan lifted her back and stood in front of Lily while she pulled her pants up.

"Mrs. Tulley?" Dale asked. Elizabeth was wearing the light, sundress that came less than halfway down her thighs. "Shona and I can hold you secure if you need to go."

Elizabeth dissolved into tears. "I can't! I just can't!" Dale tried not to let his disgust show as urine started to stream down the hysterical woman's legs.

"You can come here and help me," Keith called from where he sat, his leg propped up out of the water.

Shona started forward, but Dale caught her arm. "I'll do it."

"I need to take a shit," Keith sneered.

"Of course you do." Dale lifted Keith's leg down and took some pleasure from the way Keith hissed at the touch of the water on his wound. Embracing his boss in a rough bear hug, Dale lifted Keith up and let his weight lean on to him.

"Don't drop me," Keith snarled. Keith fumbled with his shorts, forcing them down. Dale helped the wounded man work his backside over the edge of the inflatable side.

Keith sighed and relaxed. Warm urine splashed over Dale's legs and he jerked his head back.

"Watch it," he warned.

Keith smiled. "Don't piss me off, mate." He grunted and the

stink of his bowels moving wafted over Dale.

"You're a real prick, Keith," Dale muttered.

"Wanna wipe my arse?" Keith asked.

Dale yanked Keith forward, sending the larger man's full weight down on his injured leg. Keith let out a howl of pain as he fell on Dale. Behind them, a shark's head snapped on empty air and the fish crashed back into the water.

"You fucking cunt!" Keith snarled. His fists struck at Dale who tried to protect his face while breathing through the stabbing pain in his ribs.

"Shark! There was a fucking shark!" Shona tackled Keith and knocked him aside. He slid across the wet floor, almost plunging into the hole in the rubber deck.

"Shark…" Dale groaned.

"What…?" Keith looked confused, and then pushed himself away from the hole as if expecting another attack to come bursting through it at any moment.

"There was a fucking shark," Shona repeated.

Keith realized his pants were still down around his ankles. He pulled them up, wincing at the pain in his thigh. "I'm gonna fucking die out here," he whined.

"Not necessarily," Logan announced. "Salt water solution can be good for wounds. Though a deep puncture like yours is more likely to become infected."

"You'll get gangrene and we'll have to cut your leg off," Dale said. It felt good to see the fear flood Keith's face.

"Given our lack of tools and the proximity of the wound to the torso, I think that any gangrene infection would kill Keith faster than we could hope to save him. Septicemia, a poisoning of the blood." Logan could have been giving a lecture to medical students for all the emotion in his voice.

"I'm going to see you go to jail for this, you stupid bitch." Keith wormed his way over to the edge of the life raft. He leaned back against the inflatable side and caught his breath. Elizabeth ignored him; she seemed to be singing softly under her breath, her gaze fixed on some distant horizon that only she could see.

They all sank into their own quiet misery, and soon even Elizabeth stopped singing. Shona divided their evening meal and distributed the second water ration of the day.

Darkness fell at the end of the fifth day on the life raft. Dale took first watch; surely they were getting close to the commercial shipping lanes now? He stared for hours into the endless darkness. His head throbbed with a dehydration headache, and he saw flashes of light that might have been a distant lightning storm, a ship's light, or just a hallucination.

Keith was right; if they weren't rescued soon, he would die. Shona nudged him awake at four in the morning.

"My turn," she said. Dale nodded, staying where he was, knees resting in the sloshing water, arms folded into a pillow on the edge of the life raft. He put his head down and went back to sleep.

Shona's yell woke them up an hour later. She was standing up, balancing on the shifting surface and staring hard into the pre-dawn glow.

"Ship!" she yelled again.

Dale clambered to his feet. Behind him, Logan and Lily cheered. Elizabeth burst into tears and Keith stared out across the seascape.

"See it?" Shona asked. Dale nodded; no lights, but it was definitely a ship. The silhouette of it stood out against the dawn sky.

"We're saved. It's going to be okay." Dale floundered through the water and found the flare gun. Cracking it open, he slammed a flare cartridge into it, and stood up again. Extending his arm upwards, he pointed the gun at the sky and squeezed the trigger. Nothing happened.

"Fuck!" he yelled. Opening the gun, he pulled the flare out and rubbed the base of it on his shirt. "It should just fucking work!" he yelled.

"Can you trigger it by hand?" Keith asked.

"Did it somehow get wet?" Logan piped up.

"Hey! Over here!" Shona yelled, waving her arms.

"Oars!" Dale shouted over the noise. "There are oars strapped to the outside. Grab one and start paddling!"

Logan and Lily detached the oars and soon had the wallowing life raft moving.

"Get the cover down!" Dale pulled the tabs and unfastened the heavy canvas cover of the inflatable boat. It was a Day-Glo orange, and he and Shona started waving it like a flag.

They were drifting closer to the ship. Dale couldn't see any lights on the deck or in the wheelhouse. The whole thing looked like it had seen better days. Nevertheless, it was a ship and that meant rescue.

"Keith! Untie the sea anchor. That rope over there!" Dale waved with a free hand. Keith dragged himself to the side of the life raft and untied the rope that hung over the side. The sea anchor was meant to work as a kind of rudder, keeping them on a straight course. It floated under the surface, causing drag and slowing the boat down. After it was released, the efforts of the rowers noticeably increased.

"I think we are getting closer!" Shona yelled. Dale did some mental calculations, given the slow speed of the life raft and the slow speed of the ship, and their angles... it would be a close thing.

With an eye out for sharks, he leaned over the side, adding his hand to the work of the oars.

Shona kept waving and yelling as inch by painful inch the distance between the life raft and the ship reduced. Dale could see that it was Russian. The name of the ship was written in the weird Russian script, and then in English on the bow. *Mikhail Lazarov.*

What the fuck was a Russian ship doing this far south? It wasn't a fishing trawler. It looked like a small cruise ship. Something he would have thought might be cruising around the Mediterranean or Caribbean, not out here in the Pacific.

The ship showed storm damage, salt and rust covered most of its surface. There were no signs of people, and Dale had a sinking feeling that maybe it was a drifting wreck.

He stopped paddling and stood up, staring at the approaching ship. "It's adrift. Abandoned," he said to Shona.

"What?" she was still waving and yelling herself hoarse.

"The ship, it's drifting. Probably got dumped somewhere and now it's here."

"No reason not to get on board. There might be food, a radio. Medical supplies."

Dale nodded. "Paddle, guys!"

"How are we to get on board?" Lily called out. "I don't see any ladder."

Shona stopped waving and dived under the flapping canopy. She re-emerged a moment later with the rope. "Flare gun," she said.

Dale handed it to her. Shona tied the rope around the gun and held it up. "If we can throw this up there, it could work as a grappling hook."

"Are you sure that will hold a person's weight?" Logan asked.

"I really don't think we have any choice," Shona replied and handed the rope to Dale.

The ship was drifting past them; within a few minutes, it would be gone, forever out of reach. Dale balanced carefully and swung the rope in a circle, building up momentum before letting it fly.

The flare gun clanged against the steel side of the ship and dropped into the water. Dale frantically pulled it back in.

"Try again," Shona said, her eyes intense with a desperate need.

He swung the rope again, letting it play out in a longer arc with a faster spin before it flew off. They all watched as the flare gun rose into the air, and then angled over the rail. As soon as the rope went limp, Dale started drawing it back. The rope caught on something. Dale tugged it and then yanked harder. "Okay, it's secure."

Using the rope, they pulled the life raft up against the side of the ship.

"How do we climb that?" Keith demanded.

"We don't. I do," Dale replied.

"No, let me." Shona put her hand on the thin rope. "I'm better at climbing than you and I'm lighter."

Dale didn't argue; the idea of heights made his head spin. Shona leaned back on the rope, feeling the pressure build as it took her weight. Carefully, she moved a hand up and, using her arms, she placed her feet against the steel side of the ship.

Her muscles strained as Shona crept up the side of the ship. The steel hull had no grip for her feet; the crusted salt and patches of rust were the only non-slick parts.

After twenty feet, almost halfway up the ship's side, Shona's feet slipped. She spun on the rope and slammed into the side of the hull hard enough to lose her grip on the rope. She screamed and dropped into the water, a large splash marking the spot she landed.

Dale yelled and only Logan grabbing his arm stopped him diving in after her. Shona bobbed to the surface, her face constricted with pain. "Fuck that stings!" she wailed.

"*Shark!*" Elizabeth screamed. Dale's blood went cold.

The dorsal fin broke the water a hundred yards away. Dale and Logan both leaned over the side, yelling to Shona for her to swim. Dale could see by her expression that Shona had hurt herself in the fall. Maybe scraped some skin off on the coarse rust. Either way, blood in the water meant she was in real trouble.

Shona started for the boat, her arms cutting through the water with the same athletic ease of the shark that was closing in behind her. Lily appeared next to Logan, the oar she held waving as she used it for balance. Dale grabbed Shona's outstretched hand and heaved her out of the water. The shark's mouth yawned wide where she had been a moment before. Lily smacked the creature on the side of its snout with the flat end of the oar.

"Owwww…" Shona whined through clenched teeth. The skin on her right thigh had been scraped off and blood oozed from the raw graze.

"It's okay, babe." Dale comforted his girlfriend, not mentioning the shark, or how close it came to tearing her in half.

Without a word, Dale took hold of the rope and started climbing. His ribs and chest immediately protested. He could hardly breathe, but the adrenalin of Shona's brush with death gave him the strength to keep going. After less than two minutes, he crawled onto the deck of the *Mikhail Lazarov* and lay there, gasping for air.

CHAPTER 6

Dale waved to the anxious faces below, assuring them that he was okay. He vanished from view, returning a minute later with a rolled-up rope ladder. After securing it to the rails by a pair of locking hooks, he dropped the coiled rope over the side. Lily clambered up the ladder like a monkey and stood looking around the deck while Dale called encouragement down to Elizabeth as she climbed up.

Every creak and twist of the rope ladder sent Elizabeth into hysterics. It took ten minutes of careful coaxing to get her within reach of Dale and Lily. Once she was on board, Elizabeth sat with her back against a wall and her knees drawn up.

"Logan, come on up, old man," Dale called down. Logan waved with his good hand and began the arduous climb, while keeping his burned hand out of contact with anything but the dry air.

Lily and Dale pulled him the last few rungs, and though he was pale and shaking, he managed a grin and a one-armed hug for Lily once he was on the deck.

Shona had finished bagging up their few supplies. She helped Keith get to his feet and start up the ladder. He made a trial of it; moaning every time he moved his injured leg. Keith swore with every step, threatening Elizabeth with the ass reaming that awaited her from his lawyers.

No one stepped forward to help Keith as he grunted and labored his way from the rope ladder onto the deck. He rolled over, breath hissing through his teeth as he lay on his back.

"I'll come down and get the supplies," Dale called to Shona.

"Nah, it's all good," she called back.

With the heavy bag slung over her shoulder, she swung onto the rope ladder and started climbing. The now-empty life raft looked half-sunk with seawater flushing through it.

Dale looked back at Shona as she cursed. The bag had slid off her shoulder, and landed with a splash. She hurried down a few rungs and reached for it. Slipping her hand through the canvas straps, she wrapped them around her wrist to secure the grip.

Looking up, Shona grinned at Dale, he grinned back. She had it all under control. No worries.

From his perspective, looking down from the rail of the ship, forty feet away, the final moments were clear as a series of photographs. A massive grey-white shape came up through the dark blue, pushing a bell curve of water in front of it. The shark was so large it framed Shona from behind. Her blonde hair, white teeth, and shining blue eyes, looking into Dale's with love and determination. As the shark breached, the water cascaded in a smooth sheet, barely turning to foam, so smoothly did it break the surface. The massive jaws were open, and Dale could see deep into the beast's gullet. The pastel salmon pink of its insides. The picket-fence-like points of its many teeth.

He drew breath to scream, his face contorting in terror. A shadow passed over Shona's face, and in that freeze-frame series of moments, the shark rose up, and snapped its jaws on the bag in Shona's hand. The fish would have been at least eighteen feet long. It twisted away, dragging the heavy nylon fabric of the bag and pulling Shona off the ladder. Her hand and wrist still tangled in the carrying strap. She hit the water for the second time in less than an hour. Screaming her name, Dale scrambled for the ladder.

Looking down as he descended, Dale saw the water flood with a dark color. A strange shade of almost brown, it poured up from somewhere deep. In the middle of the spreading slick, the bag popped to the surface. Battered and torn, Shona's severed hand was still caught in the carrying handle. The bag floated there, bobbing in the suddenly turbulent sea as the sharks tore and feasted. The life raft shuddered as the frenzied sharks attacked anything in the water. More of its inflatable sections popped and hissed. Sharks passed under Dale, corpse grey and bone white. He felt completely powerless. Too weak to even climb back up the ladder. He just clung there. Every muscle in his body had clenched too tight to let him fall to his death with the woman he loved.

CHAPTER 7

"Alright, everybody who can walk, I suggest we pair up and explore." Logan had his lecturing voice on again. Logan had gone down the rope ladder and talked Dale into climbing up. Dale had grabbed the floating bag as it drifted past, his face a blank mask of deep shock. Now he sat where they left him, sitting at the rail, legs hanging over the side, staring down into the water where Shona had vanished.

Logan shook him by the shoulder. "Come on, Dale. You and me, we'll check the bridge. Lily, can you take Elizabeth and head up to the front of the boat?"

"Right," Lily said. "Up we get, Elizabeth, there's work to be done." Elizabeth stood up and Lily took her hand. Together, they headed off towards the bow of the ship.

Dale still hadn't moved, so Logan crouched and lifted him by his armpits. The pain in his burned hand was excruciating. Turning the boy to face him, Logan took a breath and then slapped Dale across the face. The younger man blinked, his face flushing with furious color.

"We can all grieve later. Right now though, I need you to be focused on helping us survive."

Dale blinked again, his hand came up and touched the reddening print on his cheek. "That really hurt," he said.

"Pain is how you know you are still alive," Logan said.

"Well then I must be fucking immortal," Keith called out. "You're not going to leave me here?"

"I don't see how we have much choice." Logan turned to look at Keith.

"I can walk," Keith insisted.

"Dale, can you give me a hand? Let's see if we can help Keith stand up."

For once, Keith made an effort and they got him standing, one foot off the ground, his swollen thigh unable to bear weight. The cloth strip tied around Keith's wounded thigh dug into his puffy flesh like a ring on a fat man's finger.

"Fuck," he said.

"Hold him there, I'll find a crutch." Logan walked away, leaving Dale and Keith like a pair of ballroom dancers caught in a half-step, holding each other in an uncomfortable closeness.

Neither man spoke for several minutes, Dale was lost in the shock of his sudden grief, while Keith didn't have anything comforting to say.

Eventually, Logan returned with a mop. "Try this. It's not a perfect solution, but it should help you hobble about."

Keith took it and experimented with hopping. "This is shit. Find a damn radio or a satellite phone. Get us some goddamned help," he said.

"An excellent suggestion." Logan smiled and nodded in agreement. "Dale, I think the bridge would be the best place to start, don't you?"

"Sure," Dale said.

They left Keith red-faced with strain and muttering under his breath as he shuffled along the deck.

"Stairs to the bridge would be inside?" Logan asked.

"I guess." Dale barely looked up.

Logan rummaged in the salvaged bag and retrieved a flashlight and two more flares. "This way then," he spoke with a forced cheerfulness that seemed impervious to the gloom and misery of those around him. The doctor led Dale to the nearest door, a rusting steel portal with a round window of thick glass set in it. The crust of salt and grime had clouded the window and the rusted hinges screamed when they pulled the door open.

"Phew." Logan wrinkled his nose. The air inside carried a scent of old rot and abandoned spaces. The doctor stepped inside; the light grew dim in the corridor after a few steps. Dale followed, their silhouettes casting heavy shadows in the gloom.

Logan clicked the flashlight on and the darkness melted away in the white beam.

Dust and salt had combined to make a thin crust of grime that covered everything. The ship creaked and groaned in the steel infrastructure as they moved deeper inside. On this level, wood paneling still gleamed with varnish, and under the dust, the chrome of the railings shone.

Nearer to floor level, the wooden panels had a frayed look. Logan frowned and leaned over, peering closely. He could see teeth marks where the wood had been gnawed up to a foot above the floor. The scattering of rat droppings and tracks in the dust made him uneasy.

"Stairs," Dale said. He nodded towards a staircase that had been stripped of its wood paneling. Only a rusting metal framework remained and they stepped carefully to avoid falling into the gaps.

"Those salvage crews certainly don't leave much behind," Logan said.

Dale climbed without looking up. "They usually only take the electronics and anything re-usable. The rest is scrap."

"Most of the wood trim has been ripped down." Logan reached the top of the stairs and eyed the stripped floor with a frown. Whatever carpet or floor covering had lain here was gone. The floor now showed its rusting steel plates.

A metal door with Cyrillic writing and the English script label of *BRIDGE* identified the room they were looking for.

Behind the door, the room had been gutted. Empty steel shelving units remained like dry bones after the meat had been stripped away. A few strands of colored wire hung like tufts of hair. The entire room seemed derelict.

Logan's nose wrinkled. "Jesus, it stinks in here."

Dale shrugged. "It's probably us?"

"No, it's rotten meat." Logan moved into the bridge, sniffing lightly as he homed in on the source of the stench.

Dale followed and they stopped in front of a metal locker. "Dead rat or something?" Dale put a hand to his face to block the smell.

Logan frowned and twisted the locker handle. It resisted and he yanked on it. On the second jerk, the door popped open, and a thick slime of grey-green ooze ran out onto the floor.

"Fuck me," Dale yelped. In the dim light, they saw a child-sized corpse. Rats had chewed on the small body and the remains were rotting into foul soup.

"Where the hell did that come from?" Logan said while coughing on the stink.

"Shut the fucking door." Dale backed away, waving at the flies that had followed the smell into the bridge.

Logan used his foot to swing the locker door shut as a rat pushed its wet head out through the putrefying stomach. The door bounced open and Logan yelped as a brown bundle dropped from a shelf. Catching it, Logan hurried off the bridge, Dale stumbling ahead of him and down the stairs. They got their bearings and headed out onto the deck. Dale threw up over the side, while Logan stood by, pale and shaking.

"What's wrong with him?" Keith yelled from where he sat, leaning against the ship's steel wall.

"Just some dead rats, stinking the place up," Logan called back.

"Pussy," Keith sneered.

"Why is there a dead kid on this ship?" Dale moaned.

"I don't know," Logan replied. "I suggest we don't tell the others. They are upset already, let's not add to their stress."

"Fuck him." Dale spat the taste of sour-acid from his mouth. "He should be dead. Not Shona."

Logan put a hand on Dale's shoulder. "Easy, son. There's going to be a lot of time for grief and anger. Right now, we need to focus on staying alive. That means all of us."

Dale shuddered. "Souvenir?" He nodded at the bundle Logan still carried.

"Ah, yes. It fell off a shelf, scared the hell out of me."

They examined the brown leather package; it was an old-style leather school satchel, soft and worn with the passing of decades. The strap on it had showed signs of being sucked and chewed.

"I used to have a bag like this when I was a lad," Logan said.

He slung the strap over his shoulder, letting the bag sit on his hip.

"Anything in it? Food or a radio maybe?" Dale asked.

A scream from the bow of the ship cut through the air, interrupting their investigation.

"I think that was Elizabeth." Logan dashed ran along the deck, Dale lurching after him.

At the corner of the cabin, Logan collided with Lily who was running the other way. They both went down with a cry and Lily sprang up again. "Help," she gasped. "Someone grabbed Elizabeth."

"What?" Logan and Dale both asked.

"Hurry," Lily insisted. "They took her inside the ship."

She led the two men across the deck in front of the bridge. Dale could see scuff marks in the grime and rust, and a few dark stains that he hoped weren't blood.

"Who took her?" Logan demanded.

"I don't know." Lily stopped outside a steel door with a dark porthole in the center.

"What did they look like?" Dale wondered if Lily was suffering from some kind of hallucinations.

"Ahh, tall and thin. Close to Logan's age. He was dressed in rags and had a necklace that rattled. Oh, and he had a knife. Odd looking thing, like one of those shivs you hear about in prisons."

Dale wanted to ask how Lily knew about prison weaponry design, but Logan was talking. "Did he say anything?"

"No. He really was the oddest-looking fellow." Lily had sounded more startled than scared. Now she seemed intrigued. "Do you think he might be a pirate?"

"Modern pirates tend to drive high-speed boats, carry automatic weapons, and do hit-and-runs. They take crew and passengers for ransom," Dale said. "They also operate closer to shore."

"Maybe he was left behind when the other pirates did their hit-and-run?" Lily suggested.

"Dale, help me with this door." Logan stepped past Lily and Dale joined him as they both leaned on the handle, which remained jammed in a closed position.

"I can't see how he went in there, unless he locked it behind him," Logan panted.

"We'll go round, find another way in." Dale headed back down the deck.

Logan hesitated, "Are you all right, my dear?"

Lily smiled at him. "I'm fine, darling. We are having quite the adventure." She kept smiling as Logan nodded and followed Dale.

Looking up, she stared into the deep-set eyes of the man crouched behind the upper deck rail. He was dressed in rags, his hair and beard dreadlocked with filth and salt. He held a human thighbone, the shaft wrapped in plastic to form a grip and the club-like end dented from repeated blows. They stared at each other for several seconds, neither blinking. Then as silently as he had appeared, the man vanished from view.

CHAPTER 8

"Elizabeth?" Logan called in the dim interior of the ship. There were no remaining interior doors; even the soft furnishings were gone, everything stripped to bare metal. In places, pieces of furniture frame were missing. Further down the corridor, Dale pulled the ignition tab on a flare. The red flame sputtered into life and sent blood-toned shadows dancing along the walls.

"Elizabeth?" Logan shouted again. The ship creaked around them, moving on the currents and light swell. Dale's burning light dimmed as he descended a staircase. Logan hurried after him, rushing to keep ahead of the all-consuming darkness.

A shadow moved to his left, bringing Logan up short. He peered through an open doorway. "Elizabeth? Is that you?" With a few seconds before Dale's light walked out of range, Logan ducked into the side corridor.

The ship had once been luxurious, designed to provide a deluxe cruise experience for rich Russians and other European tourists. At the end of the side corridor, a room that might once have been a restaurant opened out. Logan stood on the threshold, unable to see anything in the dark.

"Hello?" His voice echoed in the empty space.

The slapping sound of bare feet on bare metal approached at

a light-footed run. Logan tensed and then a skull face loomed in front of him. The bones were a mask, and even in his shock, Logan knew that the skull was real, probably an adult male. Broken in a horizontal line under the eye sockets, the frontal bone resting like a hat on the bizarre figure's head and the skull mask tied on with plastic string.

"On tebya sozheret zazhivo!" the skull-faced character rasped.

"What?" Logan managed.

"He eats you. He eats you alive," skull face said with a thick Russian accent. The mad visage vanished into the darkness, Logan listening to the pattering of its bare feet on the floor.

His nerve failed him and he ran. Rushing out of the room in a blind panic, he stumbled down the stairs, shouting for Dale.

A fresh flare sparked in the darkness and Dale appeared under it, bathed in garish red light.

"Logan!"

"There are people. On this ship! People."

"What the hell is going on here?" Dale turned around in the corridor. "Hello? Is there anyone there? We could use some help!"

They stood under the sputtering light of the flare, straining to hear a response.

"C'mon, we need to find Elizabeth." Dale walked out of the empty room and Logan hurried after him, suddenly afraid of the dark.

CHAPTER 9

The smoke from the burning flare covered the smell of seawater and rot on the lower cabin deck. Logan squinted into the gloom. "There's no way she came down here, is there?"

"Elizabeth?" Dale called into the darkness. "Can you hear me?"

They stood halfway down a flight of stairs where oil-stained black water slopped against the carpet. Beyond this point, the ship had flooded.

"This could be local," Dale suggested, "if the bulkheads were secured when the water came in. They sealed the leak; otherwise, the ship would have sunk."

"Maybe the leak is recent?" Logan replied. "We could be sinking slowly now."

The two men fell silent and peered at the lagoon, watching a dark lump sending ripples across the surface as it moved through the water.

"Is that a rat?" Logan asked.

Dale wanted to say it couldn't be a rat; the shape in the flooded corridor looked way too large.

The thing reached a jutting ledge of metal and climbed out.

In the light of the flare, Dale saw it *was* a rat. A rat the size of a two-year-old child.

"Fuck me…"

As well as being impossibly large, the rat sported bald patches along the body where raw wounds glistened and oozed.

"What is that?" Logan couldn't believe what he was seeing.

"*That* is the biggest fucking rat I have ever seen."

The massive rodent regarded the two men with the same curiosity before vanishing into a narrow hole in the wall.

Logan released a slow breath. "I hate rats."

Dale shook his head. "How does a rat get that big?"

"Most rats, if they are given a steady supply of food, can grow to be maybe, eleven inches long and weigh about two pounds." Logan made no effort to step down into the water.

"So it wasn't a rat?"

"Well…"

Dale shivered. "Some kind of fucked-up dog? Maybe they were smuggling exotic pets or something?"

Logan didn't respond. He had seen enough rats in his life to know what they looked like. The tail on that thing had been over a foot long with a tail as thick as a man's index finger.

"There's no way Elizabeth went in there," Logan declared.

Dale nodded, and they moved back up the stairs towards the daylight and fresh air.

Behind them, the water rippled and a shape broke the surface. A man's head emerged, his hair and skin painted white, and stained with waste oil. He spat a snorkel tube out of his mouth and swam to the steps. Slipping out of the water, he crouched there, listening intently as he stroked a necklace of small bones that Logan could have identified as being from the right hand of a young boy.

The steel door above creaked open, and the voices of the two *inozemtsi* faded. The crouched figure's stomach rumbled. *No*, he thought. *Not foreigners. They were* M'yasyvo. *Meat.*

CHAPTER 10

Dale took a breath of the warm salt-laden air. His first thought was to find Shona and tell her what they had seen. The memory of her death hit him in the chest like a harpoon. He sagged against the flaking paint of the ship wall, chest heaving as he struggled for air.

"Easy now," Logan said calmly.

"Fuck, Shona's gone."

"Yes," Logan agreed. "It will take as long as it takes for you to accept that. There are no rules for grief and the pain of loss."

The pressure built in Dale's gut, a rising ball of hot anguish that exploded out in a wordless wail of horror and tears. He slid down onto his knees, his body wracked with the pain of loss and misery.

Logan waited in silence for the moment to pass. He knew Dale had a lot of strength, but Shona had been there with him every day on the yacht, and in the lifeboat. Her tragic death was a damned shame.

"Is Dale okay?" Lily came around the corner, her slight frame silhouetted against the afternoon sun.

"He's just having a moment of shock," Logan replied.

"Oh, the poor dear." Lily came closer and crouched beside the stricken man. "There, there," she said, rubbing Dale's shoulder.

"I'm sor-sorry," Dale stammered, his breath hitching in his chest.

"Quite all right," Logan said with a professional cheerfulness.

"Your pain is real," Lily said. "You own it. You don't need to apologize for it."

"Any sign of Elizabeth?" Logan changed the subject.

Lily sighed. "No, the poor thing. She's probably hiding somewhere and having a good cry."

"We should keep looking. It's not safe for anyone to be on their own."

"I can handle myself, Doctor," Lily said with a hint of crispness in her tone.

Logan smiled. "Yes, my dear. You are a cool head in any crisis."

Lily straightened up as Dale stood, roughly wiping tears away.

"Find anything interesting below decks?" Lily asked.

"Not really," Logan said, suddenly afraid to share the details with Lily.

"This section is flooded, the lower decks anyway. The ship could be sinking slowly under us."

"No radio or anything?" Lily asked.

"The bridge has been stripped. We didn't find any kind of radio room."

Dale took a deep breath and recovered his composure. "It's probably empty too. No point in leaving anything salvageable on board. I reckon this ship was being sold for scrap. The tow-lines probably snapped in a storm."

"Surely the owners will be looking for it?" Lily looked around as if expecting to see a fleet of tugboats steaming towards them.

"Needle in a haystack," Dale replied.

"The ocean is a big place." Logan nodded. "Plenty of ships go missing and drift for years. All we can hope for is that we wander into a shipping lane and see a manned vessel."

"We did find that bag," Dale said.

Logan slapped his hip with one hand, "Of course! In all the excitement, I'd forgotten about it."

Lily and Dale crowded around him as he unbuckled the straps. Inside, they found a book with thick pages and all manner of newspaper clippings and cutout images sticking out from between the leaves.

"Some kind of diary?" Lily asked.

Logan opened the book. "I think it's a scrapbook. Pictures from magazines and newspapers… It's America, landmarks, famous places, and movie stars. I can't read the writing."

"It's Russian," Lily confirmed. "The same as this ship."

Dale turned away. "So it belonged to some crew member. Not a lot of good it's going to do us."

"He's right; we should find some food and drinking water while we wait," Lily said with a firm confidence.

"I agree," Logan said. "There's nothing more we can do right now."

"We can sterilize water, if we have a fire. Food? Maybe catch some fish. We'll need to find some line, or a net." With something tangible to focus on, Dale's mood lifted. Being active always felt better than giving into the need to curl up in a fetal position and cry until he threw up. "How's Keith holding up?"

"Last time I saw him, he was asleep." Lily shrugged. "Sleep is certainly the best thing for him at the moment."

"We should check in on him. Let him know we are going to find water and food."

"There are very few supplies left from the life raft," Lily reminded them.

"As much as it pains me, I believe he should have something to eat, and drink," Logan said.

"Of course," Lily agreed. "It is important that the strongest keep up their strength. The injured will have to rely on their internal resources."

"That's kinda cold," Dale said.

"Lily was a nurse for forty years. Mostly in palliative care. She knows how strong the dying can be," Logan spoke with a gentle pride.

"I also know that some things are inevitable," Lily said.

"The supplies are with Keith." Dale walked around the corner and down the rust-stained deck. A salt-encrusted pile of bones and feathers crunched underfoot. Dale frowned; it was some kind of seabird, a big one, in a pile of white-and-brown powdery dirt that stank like dog shit.

"That's strange," Logan commented.

"No shit?" Dale replied.

"Well, yes shit." Logan crouched carefully on creaking knees. "See these remains show signs of digestion. The body was swallowed whole. Then the meat and soft tissues were digested and the bones and waste were excreted."

"Someone caught and ate a bird." Dale shrugged.

"If this had been eaten by a human, I would expect to see cracked bones, signs of gnawing. This creature was swallowed in one gulp."

"Maybe they were just really hungry?" Dale's stomach rumbled in agreement.

"Odd..." Logan stood. "It looks like a pile of snake droppings, except on a larger scale."

"Sea serpent sightings are up thirty percent this year. I read in National Geographic that it is attributed to climate change," Dale said with a flicker of a smile.

"Ah, haha," Logan snickered.

"If you boys have quite finished..." Lily trailed off.

"Yes, onwards to our dinner reservation." Logan linked arms with Lily, and Dale trailed them down the deck to where Keith lay panting in the shade.

"The fu... ha' you been?" he whispered.

"How are you feeling, Keith?" Lily asked.

"Shit." Keith's thigh had swollen to twice its normal size. The dressing over the wound was dark with seeping fluid and crusting blood.

Flies swarmed over the moisture and he waved them away.

"I'm gunna die and it's all that cunt's fault," Keith whined.

Lily ignored him and opened the bag with their few remaining water and food supplies. "We have half a bottle of water, and some broken crackers."

"A repast fit for a king," Logan said.

"Give me some water," Keith croaked. Lily took a sip from the bottle and handed it to Logan. He swallowed a small mouthful and handed it to Dale. The water was warm and seemed to soak right into his mouth, leaving barely anything to swallow.

"Give me some fucking water," Keith snarled.

Lily took the water bottle from Dale and screwed the lid back on.

"The fuck are you doing? Give it here!" Keith struggled to stand, the mop pounding on the deck as he supported his wounded leg.

"Steady on, Keith." Logan stepped in and caught the man's flailing arm.

"Water," Keith insisted.

"It won't do you any good," Lily said.

"The fuck do you know?" Keith snarled while trying to wrestle his arm free of Logan's grip.

"You're going to die, Keith." Lily spoke with a calm certainty. "Your leg is infected. We can't treat it and you can't help the rest of us survive. The best thing to do is simply let you pass."

"I am not going to fucking die!" Fury darkened Keith's cheeks. Flecks of dried spit crusted around his lips and the flies swarmed and tasted.

"Steady on, Lil'," Logan said.

Lily ignored him. "I worked for over forty years as a nurse. I spent a great deal of my time in palliative care of the dying. I know when someone is going to die. The best thing you can do is accept it with grace."

"Fuck off," Keith snarled.

"Now, there's no need—" Logan started to say. Lily stepped forward and kicked the mop away. Keith came down on his injured leg with his full weight. He let out a high-pitched shriek and collapsed. Lily crouched and picked up the mop before he could reach for it.

Holding the handle like a spear, Lily poked the stained bandage that dug deep into Keith's swollen thigh. He howled as fresh stains wet the cloth.

"Can you smell the rot? Can you smell the decay? The infection? The pus? Soon sepsis will start affecting your entire body. Your blood pressure will drop, your kidneys will start to fail, and then the rest of your organs will shut down. You're going to die. Accept it."

Logan's mouth was open and he seemed shocked by the brutality of Lily's words. Dale didn't react; he felt numb, and Keith was an asshole anyway.

Lily jabbed at Keith again, each poke of the mop handle punctuating her words. "It's because of you we are all here. It's your fault."

Logan blinked and seemed to come to his senses. He stepped forward and wrapped his arms around Lily, pulling her away from Keith. She tensed against him and then broke down into sobs. Dropping the mop, she buried her face in Logan's chest and wept.

"Steady on, love," Logan murmured.

"Cunt," Keith muttered and fainted.

CHAPTER 11

They watched the sunset as it filled the broad horizon with a raging fire of red and gold. In the long dusk, the remaining light made everything stand out in high-contrast and eerie shadows.

Lily dozed, her head resting in Logan's lap while he stroked her hair. Dale sat in silence nearby, no one speaking, each alone with their thoughts.

After recovering from his faint, Keith had moaned and cursed them until he only had the strength to whine and beg. In time, he fell silent, lost in his own world of wretched pain.

Dale climbed to his feet, his head pounding with dehydration. He took the empty water bottle and turned away, urinating a thick stream of dark yellow into it.

With a sigh, he lifted his head and stared into the shining eyes of a monster. A woman with tangled hair and deep-set blue eyes stared at him. She was dressed in rags and thin to the point of gauntness, her skin filthy with grime and bruises. Dale stared, wide-eyed in shock as the bottle dropped to the deck. With lightning reflexes, the woman snatched the bottle from the air and sniffed the contents.

"What…?" Dale croaked.

"Khoroshiy napitok?" the ragged creature whispered.

"Help…us. Please?" Dale managed.

She straightened and waved dismissively. *"Net pomoshch' dlya vas, myaso."*

Dale turned at the sound of a ragged scream from further up the deck. Terror made him look back. The strange woman had vanished into the rising darkness, taking the water bottle with her.

"Keith?" Logan called. Dale started running towards the sound of the man's screams.

The wounded man had gone from his shaded spot against the steel wall of the ship. Smeared body fluids showed a dark trail in the falling light. Dale followed it, Logan snatching up a flashlight and hurrying to catch up.

They ran along the deck, Dale's head pounding in time with the thudding of his feet on the warm steel. A steel door banged shut a second before they skidded to a halt.

"Did you see who took him?" Logan asked.

"You sure someone did?" Dale replied.

"It's not like he could run down here himself."

Dale tried the door. It resisted his efforts to twist the latch open.

"Help me."

Logan took hold of the handle and together they heaved against it. The resistance on the other side creaked and then gave way. With a wail of rusting hinges, the door swung open.

A ragged rope dangled from the handle, the frayed ends dragging in the dust.

"Christ, what is that smell?" Dale coughed and covered his nose. The stench wafting out was putrefaction and ammonia, strong enough to burn the hairs in his nose.

"Let's have a look," Logan said, and clicked the flashlight on. The beam played over the interior walls. Stick figures painted in dried blood and thick smears of shit paraded around the walls.

"There are people on board," Dale said.

"Now you believe me? It might be too much to ask that they are friendly. I can't imagine anyone choosing to live on a drifting hulk like this."

Dale could barely think straight, with the exhaustion and dehydration. "Maybe they're on some kind of extreme cruise?"

Logan just grunted and started down the stairs. Like the other interior corridors of the ship they had seen, the wood paneling, carpets, and anything else had been stripped away.

They reached the lower deck and stopped. "Which way?" Dale asked.

Before Logan could reply, a howling sound echoed along the corridor. "That way," Logan said.

The flashlight beam picked up flaking paint and the exposed ribs of the steel deck-frame. Moving as quickly as they dared, Logan and Dale moved down the corridor.

A second flight of stairs lead down into a ransacked dining room. The furniture had been scattered, and the soot from a fire in the center of the room stained the ceiling plaster.

Logan clicked the flashlight off, and they ducked down behind the bannister. The rising flames of the fire sent shadows dancing around the room. Moving through the flickering light came a trio of men. Two carried a struggling figure between them. Keith lacked the strength to put up much of a fight, mostly he whined and cursed with each ragged breath.

The third figure gestured and the two bearers dropped their load in front of the fire. As Keith struggled to sit up, they pushed him down with a few swift kicks, and then stood on his wrists to hold him down.

"Who the hell are they?" Dale whispered. Logan shook his head. The third man wore the upper half of a human skull as a mask that covered his eyes. His long hair was matted and tied with scraps of wire and braided around fragments of bone.

"Stay quiet," Logan whispered.

A glint of steel flashed in the firelight. The masked figure crouched over Keith's squirming form. A long knife shaped from beaten steel waved in a swaying rhythm. The masked figure sang deep in his throat, a growling hum, echoed by the other two.

The tip of the knife traced lines in the air over Keith's body. With each pass, the blade passed closer to his quivering skin.

With crouching steps, the masked dancer worked his way down Keith's body. The blade slid under the stained bandage and Keith shrieked. With a jerk of the knife, the cloth parted and was peeled away.

"Help me," Keith whispered.

"Daaa...Daaa..." the swaying figure moaned. The blade scraped over the swollen flesh of Keith's thigh. Pressing deeper into the skin, then breaking it like a knife slipping through the icing on a rich cake.

Keith screamed, his body flexing in a spasm of agony as he struggled to escape.

The man with the knife continued his work, slicing fevered flesh down to the knee. With a practiced ease, the knife turned and sliced around Keith's leg and up the other side. A ring of blood swelled and wept in the blade's wake.

After a few cuts, Keith's leg lay open like the cover of a book. The butcher worked the knife around the bone, cutting the meat away, and leaving Keith's living bone glistening in the firelight. Keith fainted with a barely audible sigh.

Dale swallowed his nausea while Logan stared, wide-eyed and open-mouthed in shock.

The butcher bound the open wound at the top of Keith's thigh with a tourniquet of wire. Twisting it until the flesh bulged and the gushing blood slowed to a seeping ooze.

Satisfied that nothing would be wasted, the man threaded the chunk of meat onto a length of wire and hung over the glowing embers of the fire. The smell of roasting meat made Dale's mouth water and his nausea grew stronger.

"Holy shit…" Dale whispered.

"I can't believe it… This is insane." Logan shook his head and stared at the horrific scene going on below them.

"Logan?" Lily emerged from the darkness behind them.

"Fuck." Dale jumped. Her silent approach nearly stopped his heart.

"What's going on?" Lily sank into a crouch as Logan waved her down.

"There are people on the ship," Logan whispered. "They have killed Keith."

"Oh, how?" Lily crept forward to get a better look.

"How?" Dale echoed. "There's fucking crazed cannibals on board and you want to know how they killed Keith?"

"Keep your voice down," Logan whispered.

Lily peered through the railing and studied the scene next to the fire. "They must have Elizabeth too."

"We should try and reason with them. See if they have any way of summoning help." Logan clung to reasoning like it was a life-preserver in a storm-tossed ocean.

"What language is that?" Lily whispered.

"I don't fucking know," Dale replied.

"I think, it's Russian," Lily continued, ignoring Dale.

Logan nodded. "This is a Russian ship. We found Cyrillic writing on the bridge."

"What is it doing so far from Russia?" Lily murmured. "They are moving," she added.

Logan crept closer and looked out over the dining room. Keith was being lifted up and carried away into the darkness. The butcher lifted the roasting cut of Keith's thigh from the fire and caressed it with his fingers before licking the oily juices from them.

Lily moved silently and knelt down next to Logan. "I wonder where they are getting their essential nutrients from?"

Logan wondered the same thing, but the horror of the situation made such a clinical observation seem inhuman.

"We have to save our friend," Logan announced. He climbed to his feet, wincing slightly at the creak of his joints.

"We should be saving ourselves," Lily reminded him. Dale moved in a half-crouch, peering down into the abandoned dining room. "They've gone."

"We can't stay here," Logan said.

"You're damned right." Dale turned and glared at the older man. "You said there were people on board. I didn't get it. I didn't fucking listen. We have to find a way off this fucking ship."

"Language, please," Lily scolded. Dale just stared at her, his mouth opening in surprise.

"It's all right, Lily. Dale, we can't leave without finding Elizabeth."

"And fuck Keith, right?" Dale almost laughed.

"Keith…" Logan sighed. "Keith is not likely to survive an injury like that."

"So fuck them both. We build a raft or something, scavenge supplies and get the fuck out of here."

A shout from below captured their attention. A ragged group of gaunt people wearing a macabre mix of clothing scraps and human bones were silhouetted against the dying flames of the cooking fire.

The tableau froze for a moment, then exploded in shouts and hoots. The cannibals leapt up the walls, using holes in the decaying plasterwork and gold-painted balustrades as hand and footholds.

"Run," Lily shouted. They bolted up the corridor and onto the stairs. Logan fumbled with the flashlight, flicking it on as a howling laugh echoed around them. A flickering shadow higher on the stairs drove them back and down the corridor.

"Stairs," Dale said. He skidded on the metal floor, scrambling to maintain his balance. Logan and Lily followed on Dale's heels. Running down another flight, they descended into a smell of rotting meat and scorched plastic.

"How is this getting us out?" Logan panted.

"Hide first. Escape later," Dale replied.

Most of the doors that lined the corridor were open and the torn remains of bedding were strewn across the corridor.

Dale checked each room, dismissing the smaller cabins which had been stripped back to bare metal.

Lily continued down the corridor, Logan carrying the flashlight in her wake.

"Wait," Dale called. Muttering curses, he followed the

receding pool of light.

"We must go deeper," Lily said with a calm certainty. Logan had always admired the way she kept a cool head. As partners in their later years, they made a good team: self-possessed and comforting, with minimal demands on each other to change or adapt.

"Wait for Dale," he said and stopped hurrying.

"We should be searching these rooms," Dale said.

"There's nothing here," Lily replied. "We must go further into darkness. Beyond the easy pickings, to where angels fear to tread."

"The fuck is she talking about?" Dale asked and Logan shrugged.

Lily put her hand flat against a door. "This one."

Logan pulled on the handle, feeling it grind against salt and rust as it moved.

The howls of pursuit grew louder and flickering flames of oil-burning torches sent shadows pulsing and cavorting up the walls.

"Dale, come on." Logan pushed the door open an inch, the hinges shrieking in agony. The puff of salt-laden air that came from the darkness beyond only added to the stagnant odor in the corridor.

Dale threw himself against the scarred metal, feeling the pain of the impact wash over him.

"Nearly got it…" Logan said through gritted teeth. Dale pulled back and slammed against the door again. It popped wide enough to let Lily slip through.

"Give me the light," she said from the darkness beyond the door. Logan handed it over without question.

"Get in there," Dale snarled. Logan squeezed his thin frame through the gap. The ragged people hunting them came charging down the corridor. There were at least six of them that Dale could see. He turned and jammed his frame into the space made by the half-open doorway.

"Shit," Dale muttered as he came up hard against the press of the steel door. Inhaling, he sucked in everything and squeezed harder against the gap. The hollering and howling grew deafening. Dale rolled his eyes, blinking and trying to focus on the cloud of chaos erupting around him.

The first of the cannibals slammed a jagged blade into the steel door, inches away from Dale's arm. They screamed in delight, waving blades and feinting at Dale.

On the other side of the gap, Logan grabbed Dale's arm and tried to pull him through. More howling freaks came scampering down the corridor, waving weapons and banging on the exposed steel of the bulkheads.

"Lily! Help me here!" Logan reached past Dale's head and pulled on his shoulder.

With a yelp, Logan snatched his hand back. A gush of blood stained Dale's shirt.

"One of those buggers stabbed me!" Logan sounded more surprised than hurt.

Dale strained to get through the doorway. Another knife flicked up his cheek, laying it open, and sending a line of fire burning up his face.

A bearded face, painted in streaks of black oil and some kind of white paint, lunged into view. The man's tongue swirled over the gaping wound on Dale's cheek and dragged upwards to his hairline.

"Get the fuck away from me," Dale snarled.

"*Vy tak priyatnyy vkus*," the blood licker whispered.

His knife came up to Dale's face until the tip danced through the air near his eye.

"Going to fuck you up," the man said, his English heavily accented.

"Who the fuck are you people?" Dale asked.

"*Raby Boga*." The bearded man grinned. "Slaves of God." He turned and shouted to the others who waited like a circle of vultures for Dale to die.

"*My raby Bozh'i!*"

The corridor wheezed with the panting breath of the gathered hunters as they grinned.

Dale could see red bruises and open sores that oozed pus on the nearest of the freaks. Further away, someone coughed with the wet lungs of the terminally ill.

The bearded man kept a companionable hand on Dale's shoulder, as he grinned and nodded at the group in the corridor.

"You are fucked, yes?" he asked with that same grinning voice.

A caress on the back of Dale's head made him start. He couldn't turn to see, but he heard Lily whisper, "Get ready."

The bearded man yelled, his arm jerking away from Dale's shoulder as he stared at a long gash that suddenly welled blood from his elbow to his wrist.

In the same moment, Dale was jerked deeper into the space beyond the door. He stuck for a moment, straining with every muscle, then popped into the darkness.

The bearded man's face filled the narrow doorway. He howled in fury, slashing at them with his jagged knife.

Dale stumbled away, Logan catching him under the arms as he fell.

"Not today, you motherfucker!" Dale yelled.

Lily blocked Dale's view as Logan eased him to the floor. He heard the bearded man howl in pain. Lily stepped back and scooped up the dropped flashlight.

"Logan, close the door, please." She might have been feeling a draft for all the panic in her voice.

Logan sprang up, throwing his weight against the door as a dozen hands scrambled through the gap. Heavy steel slammed shut on their arms and screams of pain added to the cacophony of noise.

The door bounced open a few inches, and the arms retreated almost on reflex. Logan shoved a second time, and the door boomed closed.

Panting, the older man slid a locking bolt home and leaned against the steel, his eyes closed as he shuddered.

"I think we are safe. For now."

"Thank you, Logan," Lily said.

Dale sat up. "Fuck that stings." He probed the weeping gash on his face.

Lily turned the flashlight on him. "We will have to clean it and perhaps Logan can suture it for you."

"Yes… I can do that. If we can find a first-aid kit with sterile suture thread and needles."

Dale stood, wiping his hands on his blood-stained shirt. "Lily? You're bleeding?" Logan came over, his face wracked with concern.

"What? Oh, no this isn't my blood," Lily waved Logan's concern away.

Dale stared; the front of Lily's sundress was dark with blood. It looked like something from a horror movie.

"We should keep moving," Lily said.

CHAPTER 12

"We have gone behind the iron curtain," Logan mused. "I think this part of the ship is the service area. The tourists, the passengers, they would not see this part."

"I hope our Russian friends don't know another way in," Lily replied. She led the way down a moldering corridor. Salt water and air burned the metal fittings and turned the polished steel to ash-like rust.

The remaining wood here showed the same patterns of gnawing and erosion as the panels on the bridge deck. "Keep an eye out for rats," Dale said.

"Rats?" Lily asked, a quaver in her voice for the first time.

"I'm sure they are all gone," Logan said before Dale could tell her about the rat they had seen earlier.

"We must be near the bottom of the ship," Lily said.

"You mean, the hull," Dale said.

Lily glanced at him, her expression cold in the glow of the flashlight. A moment later, she relaxed and smiled at Dale. "Perhaps there might be supplies? A storeroom?"

Dale nodded. "Maybe the engine room too." He tried not to let hope take root. If they weren't lost in some sanity-straining nightmare, then he didn't need to have the last of his optimism crushed as well.

"Worth a look." Logan's calm cheerfulness acted as a balm to Dale's despair. "Lead on, oh Lady With The Lamp," Logan continued.

Lily gave a flicker of a smile and carried on, leading them deeper into the ship. Water splashed underfoot, rising to cover their shoes in a stinking layer of slime and shimmering oil. "Listen…" she announced, her head cocked to the side. Logan and Dale stopped walking in her wake, hearing only the creak and whisper of the dead ship.

"Voices," Lily continued. Dale heard it then, a chanting sound like singing or howling.

"I think it is coming from this direction." Logan pushed a door on the right side of the corridor. It swung open, the hinges oiled to silence.

The room beyond was the largest space they had seen, other than the abandoned dining room. A metal walkway ran the length of the room, disappearing into a smoky haze lit by guttering oil lamps.

Under the walkway, the room was flooded with stinking sea water. The surface rippled and writhed like it was being stirred. Overhead hung cages of large rats; they squealed and crawled over each other, eyes focused on the humans who stood staring at the nightmare menagerie.

"Rats…" Lily whispered, physically recoiling against Logan, who put a protective arm around her shoulders.

"There might be a door at the other end," Dale said, staring at the snake-filled tanks.

"We'd best keep moving," Logan replied.

A chain rattled, and the rats erupted in squeaking alarm. A cage filled with the black-and-brown vermin lowered closer to the water.

"Oh my God..." Dale managed as the surface erupted and hundreds of snakes breached the surface, their mouths gaping open.

The snakes he could see were massive, over five feet in length, with fangs like sabre-tooth cats. The bottom of the rat cage swung open, and a few rodents dropped into the water. The rest clung on to the mesh and climbed over each other in desperation.

As the rats boiled out of the open cage, and started to climb the outside of the mesh, it dropped into the tank.

The three people stood, transfixed until the cage began to rise again. The rats were gone, and the water still churned with the feasting snakes.

"Let's get the fuck out of here," Dale said. He took the flashlight from Lily, who was staring wide-eyed at the hanging rat cages. Hurrying down the gangway, Dale saw a door at the other end of the room.

"Come on," he called back. "There's a door."

"Look out!" Logan shouted. A snake with a body as thick as Dale's thigh reared up out of the water, the mouth gaping wide enough to easily swallow his head. Dale yelped and ran. The serpent's fangs crashed down on the walkway, leaving a smear of viscous fluid.

"Fucking move!" Dale yelled. He reached the door, scrambling to twist the handle and force it open. The door held, then jerked open, as if released from the other side.

Dale stumbled through, falling to his knees on the other side.

Logan followed close behind with Lily cowering under his arm as they ran.

Standing, Dale froze, two men and two women stood in a semi-circle in front of him. The crude spears they pointed at him looked sharp enough to cut through flesh and bone.

"Zakroy dver'!" one of the men snarled. His companion sprang forward and pushed the door shut before taking a position in front of it.

"Dolzhny li my ubit' ikh?" the man blocking the door asked.

"Net," one of the woman said. *"Monk budet khotet' videt' ikh."*

"I'm sorry, I don't speak… Russian?" Dale said, his hands raising slowly to his shoulders.

"You are American?" the same woman asked.

"No, Australian," Dale replied quickly.

"Australia? You are America's bitch," the woman replied.

"Well, yeah… I guess." Dale shrugged.

"Our yacht sank," Logan spoke up. "We were adrift for, well, quite some time. Then we saw this ship and I'm afraid we had little choice but to come on board."

"Shut up, old man," the woman snarled.

"We're very sorry if we did anything to upset you," Dale said. "We are just looking for our friend, Elizabeth."

"Elizabeth?" The woman nodded. *"Elizabet,"* she repeated for the others. They nodded and grinned with black teeth.

"If we can find her, we will uhh, leave," Dale said.

"Yes, you will see her. You will see everything in good time." The woman smiled, her teeth as black and foul as the others. With a jerk of her head, she indicated they should follow. Dale fell into step behind her, then Logan and Lily. The other three brought up the rear.

They passed more smoking lamps, then a curtain of rotting carpet was lifted, and they walked into some kind of temple lit with a thousand flickering flames. The walls were covered in garish murals showing figures with snakes coiling around their bodies. There were saint-like images with halos glowing over their heads and Gorgon-like drawings of women, naked and writhing in sexual ecstasy in beds of living serpents.

"Monk," the woman called. A figure stood up, tall and broad shouldered. His grey hair and beard were long and twisted into patterned braids. Naked, except for a stained pair of shorts, his visible skin was inked with complex tattoos and scars.

"We found them," the woman announced.

"Khorosho," the man growled. A snake pushed its way through the hanging tapestry of his hair and reached out to taste the air in front of him with its tongue. He lifted the snake gently and placed it in steel drum filled with water.

"Monk," the woman said and nodded towards the man.

"God has sent you," Monk intoned, his voice slow and deep. The timbre of it gave Dale a chill crawling sensation up his spine. This man was clearly bat-shit fucking crazy.

"I guess," Dale said.

"We are *Raby Boga,"* Monk replied. "We are the Slaves of God."

"I don't know what that means," Dale said.

"God made slaves of all men. This is why we suffer. We endure the torments of this world, so we may be purified for the next."

"Okay." Dale didn't know what else to say. He wished that Lily or Logan would speak up, but was afraid that if they said anything, it might get them all killed.

"We were looking for our friend, Elizabeth," Dale said.

"*Da.* The girl. She is a bride of the serpent. A vessel for absolution."

"Where is she?" Dale asked.

"It is time," Monk replied. "*Vremya prishlo.*"

The woman nodded again and pushed Dale to the side. "Do not move," she warned.

Logan and Lily were dragged forward. Monk considered them for a moment, his dark eyes never blinking. Then with a gesture, they were dismissed and pushed to stand with Dale.

Voices rose in a rhythmic chant and an unseen drum began to pound. A painted curtain parted and Elizabeth came into view. She had been stripped naked and her skin was painted in swirled patterns of dark oil. Her long hair was crudely shaved, blood oozing from scrapes and cuts on her scalp. Two similarly painted women guided her forward. Elizabeth seemed dazed, her gaze unfocused on the floor.

"Elizabeth," Logan shouted. The outburst earned him a blow between the shoulder blades. He dropped to his knees with a gasp of pain. Lily crouched to check on him.

"Please," Dale said, raising his hands. "We are just pleased to see Elizabeth is okay."

Monk arched his back, stretching the tattoos on his skin until they writhed. "She is ready to look into the face of God."

"Don't hurt her." Dale tried not to plead, but begging for Elizabeth's life was all he could do.

Monk's shoulders flexed. "If her faith is strong, God will keep her and cradle her." He turned to the watching ship-dwellers, his arms stretching wide. *"Yesli yeye vera sil'na, Bog budet derzhat' yeye i yeye kolybeli!"*

The two women laid Elizabeth down on a metal bench. She whimpered slightly at the cold steel bench that pressed against her spine. Her head hung over the end and they positioned her head over the open drum.

Monk started chanting, and Dale wondered if it was Russian, or Latin. He didn't understand either language. But the sonorous drone coming out of Monk's mouth raised the hairs on the back of his neck.

Crouching down on the other side of the drum, Monk reached out and caressed Elizabeth's skull. The blood smeared over her skin, and he pressed his hands more firmly. Drawing his arms back, she slid along the narrow bench, until her head dipped into the water.

"What are you doing?" Lily peered through the smoke and haze. Logan stood with her, holding her back or leaning against her, Dale couldn't be sure.

"Tishe!" the woman guarding Dale hissed.

Monk plunged Elizabeth's head into the drum. The water boiling as her head below the surface. Monk chanted for a long minute, and then like a baptismal preacher, he lifted Elizabeth into a sitting position.

Coiling snakes now encased Elizabeth's head in a Gorgon-like hairdo of writhing horror. Her eyes were wide, staring blindly as fresh blood trickled from her alien hairline and gathered in the sunken pits of her eyes.

"Please…" Dale whispered.

The snakes lifted from the water hissed, striking the air and each other, drops of seawater and venom scattering down Elizabeth's skin.

"*Ona dolzhna stat' sosudom yeye spaseniya.* She must become the vessel of her salvation," Monk intoned.

Elizabeth wept, her tears mixing with blood and tracing new patterns on her skin. A snake with brightly contrasted stripes rose from the knot and twisted to stare into Elizabeth's eyes. The creature's forked tongue flicked, tasting the scent of her blood and tears. It drew back and then struck with lightning speed. The fangs sank into Elizabeth's skin above her left eye. Her mouth dropped open and she moaned, her body shuddering in sudden agony.

Dale screamed and the followers of Monk howled in savage delight. After the first strike, a dozen more snakes pounced, their elongated fangs burying deep in the flesh of Elizabeth's face and neck. Her skin darkened under the pulsing injections of venom.

Before their eyes, Elizabeth's skin began to break down. The tissue turned black and split as if it were decaying at an accelerated rate. Dale shook his head, trying to wake from the nightmare. Elizabeth's eyes bulged, swelling with blood until they split. Blood poured from the woman's ruined face. Her muscles dissolved, the flesh turning to jelly and sloughing away as the snakes gorged themselves on the liquefying mess.

Logan wept and moaned in denial, his face wracked with grief and horror.

Lily merely blinked, her face expressionless and devoid of disgust or horror. Her calm demeanor made Dale want to scream.

Elizabeth's face slid away in bloody chunks, and the slick white bone of her skull leered at them for a moment until finally her body toppled backwards onto the bench.

"Oh God…" Dale croaked, his voice hoarse with shock.

"The vessel was unworthy," Monk declared.

"You murdered her! You murdered that poor woman!" Logan screamed through tears.

"We are all God's slaves, He punishes us as He sees fit," Monk replied with a shrug.

"You... are insane..." Dale gave voice to his shocked realization.

"It is God who is insane," Monk said calmly. He gestured at the watching guards, and they stepped forward and seized Dale, Logan, and Lily.

"Erzhite ikh v bezopasnosti. Ya budu zhdat' slovo Bozhiye," Monk commanded.

The three survivors were dragged from the chapel and through the curtain. The room beyond flickered with the lights of sputtering oil lamps. The acrid stench of chemicals and rotting flesh burned their tired noses. Under the close watch of the guards, the three survivors were marched into a cage. The walls and ceiling were made of salvaged lengths of metal, lashed together with wire. The entire box looked like a nightmare.

Once inside, the door was slammed and wired shut. The guards walked away, leaving the three people in stunned silence.

CHAPTER 13

"Damnit." Dale jerked his hand back and sucked the blood from his finger.

"Logan is sleeping," Lily said quietly. "Please keep your voice down."

"Cut myself on the wire," Dale muttered.

"With all that is going on, it makes sense that a cut finger is your greatest concern."

Dale frowned at Lily; there was no mockery in her expression. No sarcasm, just an icy calm.

"We need to get out of here," Dale said.

"Yes. We need to escape. We also need food, water, and medical supplies."

Dale turned and sat down with his back to the cage wall. "How can you be so calm?"

Lily looked up from where she sat with Logan's head resting in her lap. "Would you prefer that I be a damsel in distress?"

"No… It's just weird."

"You don't know anything about me, Dale."

"True, we've got time now."

"You were a nurse, right?"

"All my professional life. Before that, I was a nurse, but didn't get paid for it. My mother had polio. As her daughter, it fell to me look after her."

"Where was your father?"

Lily stared at him. "I never knew my father. My mother never spoke of him."

"Polio, that leaves you paralyzed right?"

"It can do that. The virus attacks the nervous system. Of course, since the 1950's, vaccinations against polio have almost eradicated the disease. We lived with my grandparents until they died when I was eight. After that, it was just my mother and I."

"It can't have been easy."

"Very little in life is easy, Dale. Nothing in my experience suggests otherwise."

Dale let his thoughts flow over his memories. Life had been pretty easy. Parents were okay, school had been the usual hassle. He grew up on boats and his love of sailing meant work had always been easy to come by, especially working for rich bastards on their yachts. Shona had been the icing on the cake though. Now the entire cake had been dumped on the floor and covered in dog shit.

"Which is why nursing is all I have ever known," Lily said.

"Boats," Dale replied. His eyes closing as he sighed. "I've always known boats."

Behind him, the curtain twitched, and a slight figure slipped into the room. Lily watched as she approached the cage. Dale twisted around, going to his knees as she crouched next to him.

"*Sumka,*" the women hissed.

"What?" Dale replied.

"*Sumka.* The bag," the woman insisted.

"Bag? What bag?"

"She wants the bag you have been carrying around with you," Lily explained.

The woman nodded and started untwisting the wires that held the door shut.

Logan stirred and sat up. "What's going on?"

"It's all right, dear, we have an unexpected guest."

"We have to get out of here," Dale whispered. The woman nodded. The wire catch parted, and she jerked the cage door open.

"I saw you on the deck," Dale said.

"*Da,*" she nodded. "*Alyona.* I am Alyona."

"Dale, Lily, and the old man is Logan."

"Good for you, now shut up and follow me."

Outside their prison, they followed Alyona's lead. She climbed up onto the cage and pulled a ventilation screen aside.

"Hurry," she whispered. Wriggling like a snake, she vanished into the ceiling. Dale went to hoist Lily up, but she stopped him with a glare. Climbing easily, she vanished after Alyona.

"You okay to climb, Logan?"

"I'm not dead yet." Logan gave a weak smile. He climbed slowly and with care. Dale's nerves were ragged by the time the older man wormed his way into the shaft.

Checking that the bag was secure, Dale followed them. A couple of feet into the ceiling space, the shaft turned on a right angle and ran parallel to the deck.

Following Logan's feet, Dale emerged into a small chamber stuffed with the remnants of clothes and bedding.

Lily sat cross-legged next to Alyona and sipped water from a plastic bottle.

"Water?" Dale croaked. Alyona handed him a second bottle. The contents were brackish and tasted of plastic, but to Dale, it was better than the coldest beer he had ever tasted on a summer's afternoon.

Logan shared Lily's bottle while Alyona tugged on the leather satchel Dale carried.

"Where you find this?" Alyona demanded.

"Ah, on the bridge? It was in a locker."

"Locker? Where is Alexi?"

"Who the hell is Alexi?"

"My brother. This is his bag." Alyona flipped the satchel open and extracted the scrapbook. "Alexi love America."

"We're Australians," Dale said with a hint of apology.

"There was a body. A young lad," Logan said. "Near the satchel. I'm sorry, but he had been dead for some time."

Alyona folded up, her head pressing against the scrapbook as she sobbed, her shoulders wracked with grief.

"I'm sorry," Dale said.

Alyona took a deep breath, straightening up and squaring her shoulders. "I knew him to be dead. Searched for him a long time. Alexi, always so good at hiding."

Lily spoke up. "Can you tell us who those others are? They called themselves the Slaves of God?"

"Monk," Alyona spat the name. "I promised Alexi a new life in America. Escape from everything turning to shit in Crimea."

"You're Crimean?" Logan raised an eyebrow.

"*Da*. After Russian army invade; things go badly for us in Sevastopol. Alexi and I want new life in America. We pay man to smuggle us to Istanbul. Then we go on ship. They say it go to

Canada. Canada close to America.”

“What happened? How did you end up here?”

Alyona shrugged. “Ship abandoned by crew at India. Other ship tow across ocean. Big storm. Other ship disappears, now we here.”

“How long ago was that?” Lily asked.

Alyona shook her head. “After Russian make Crimea part of Russia again.”

“That was in 2014,” Logan said. “You’ve been drifting for two years?”

“Seem like lifetime.”

“Where did the crazy fucking cult come from?” Dale asked.

“You mean Monk? *Bravta*. Russian Mafia. He *lyudi kontrabandist*. Smuggle people. Tell us we have new life in America. He go crazy. Start talking to God. People believe him and he make rules now.”

“Jesus fucking Christ.” Dale swallowed more water. “We are so fucking-fucked.”

“*Da*,” Alyona replied.

“We could kill him,” Dale said. “Sneak up on the cunt and fucking kill him.”

“Monk have God on his side. The snakes be his sign. Monk talk to snake. Make snake obey. Snake warn Monk if you come to kill him. Snake kill you.”

“We saw what they can do,” Lily said. “I had no idea snake venom could do that to human tissue.”

Logan cleared his throat. “It can’t. These are sea snakes. There are different species, but only a few can possibly be fatal to humans. What we saw… that was something unnatural.”

“So you think that this Monk arsehole has a hotline to God?”

"No, I'm not saying that at all." Logan's face turned serious. "There is something very different about these snakes. And what about that rat we saw? It was huge and looked like it was afflicted with some terrible cancer."

"A fucking rat smokes too much and gets cancer. Who gives a fuck?" Dale waved his arm and narrowly avoided banging his elbow on the metal wall.

"Did you see those drums that Monk was keeping the snakes in?"

"No, I was too busy watching Elizabeth get her head chewed off."

"It may be nothing," Logan pressed on. "They were chemical drums. The symbol on them was a red diamond with a human silhouette in the center and some kind of star?"

"So what?"

"It's the international symbol for chemicals known to be carcinogenic or mutagenic."

"We're trapped in a floating toxic waste dump. Fucking great."

"Exposure to those chemicals could have caused mutations in successive generations of snakes and rats."

"A mutation that may have caused gigantism in rats and a massive increase in the toxic concentration of the snakes?" Lily asked.

"It's just a theory," Logan said.

"Shit…" Dale breathed.

"Under us. Ship all flooded. Down there, all snakes. Bigger than man. Eat you whole," Alyona said.

"No, that's impossible," Logan replied.

"God make all things possible, yes?"

Dale wiped the sweat from his face. "Okay, we just stay out of the flooded decks and avoid the crazy man-eating motherfuckers."

"You want get off ship?"

"Yes, we would like that very much," Logan said.

"I make boat. It hide down deep."

"You have a boat?" Lily asked. "Why are you still here if you have a way off this ship?"

"I could not leave, not without Alexi."

"We can leave now then. You have Alexi's scrapbook," Lily said.

"Da…" Alyona sighed.

CHAPTER 14

Alyona gathered her supplies and led them down one of four narrow shafts that converged on the nest. They dropped out into an empty corridor, knee-deep in a fast flowing current.

"You think anyone will ever believe our story?" Dale whispered.

"We might be the lead on the news for a few days. Someone will make a movie. Then we will be forgotten," Logan replied.

"I'd sooner not tell," Lily said quietly.

"Lily values her privacy," Logan explained.

"You apologize for her a lot, you know," Dale said.

Logan smiled and gave a slight shrug. "No one is perfect. Except in the eyes of those who love them."

"She's kinda cold, mate."

"Lily has experienced many difficulties in her life. I find it best not to judge people."

"Quiet," Alyona hissed at them.

The corridor ended at a ragged hole where the steel panels of the floor had collapsed into the darkness. The water washing around their legs flowed in a tumultuous waterfall into the void.

Alyona stood at the edge and studied the abyss. Lifting a coil of woven rope, she threw a weighted end over an exposed beam. Lily grabbed Alyona's arm as the girl overbalanced catching the swinging rope.

Dale blinked; Lily's reflexes were another thing about her that gave him the creeps.

"Steady now," Lily said. Alyona righted herself and jerked her arm from Lily's grip.

"We go down," Alyona said. She tied the rope off and vanished into the waterfall, descending hand-over-hand.

"We don't know what is down there," Dale warned. Lily ignored him. Grabbing the twisting rope, she wrapped her feet around it and began to climb down.

"After you," Dale said to Logan.

Logan took a deep breath and followed Lily down the rope. Dale stood alone in the fast-moving stream. Following Alyona was insane. Their entire situation was insane. Staying here, alone, that was fucking certifiable.

The rope swung loosely until Dale caught it, his feet hanging free as he used the strength of his arms to hold his weight on the way down.

Freezing water blinded and half-choked him until he felt the deck under his feet. Alyona appeared like a watery apparition and pulled him out of the flood.

"That was fun, let's go again," Dale managed.

"Stay close, not die," Alyona replied.

The water was deeper down here, but other than the chaos of the waterfall, it was still.

Alyona took Dale by the hand and dragged him through the water. "Step careful. Deep hole," she warned.

Dale felt the steel beams under his feet and the emptiness of the spaces in between. The idea of snakes coming up from the dark water and biting him with venom toxic enough to melt the muscles off his legs nearly froze him in place.

He kept going, stepping on Alyona's heels until she stepped up onto a ledge above the level of the water.

"Logan? Lily?" Dale called into the dark.

"Here," Logan called back.

"Everyone okay?" Dale asked.

"We're fine, Dale." Lily sounded amused.

Alyona stepped past them and pushed a rusting door open. "This way," she said. Without the flashlight, they moved in complete darkness. The Russian girl moved with certainty and sparks flashed until she struck a flame to an oil lamp.

"Here I make boat," she said.

Dale opened his mouth to laugh, then closed it again. Her boat was barely a raft. A lashed-together collection of aluminum and plastic tubes and the surviving remnants of their inflatable life boat bundled up next to it.

"Sail to America," Alyona announced, her dark teeth flashing in the flickering light.

"Sure, why not." Dale grinned back.

"How do we get it out of here?" Lily asked.

"There is… hole… ways to get to deck. Hide boat up there until it is time," Alyona explained.

Under her directions, they gathered up the parts of the raft and carried it out to the ledge. Alyona went ahead, trailing a cord to the rope under the waterfall. Climbing up, she dragged the tied bundle up and out of sight.

"Why did she bring us down here?" Lily asked.

"Hey!" Dale yelled into the darkness. "You still there?"

They waited in silence, senses straining to hear anything over the roar of falling water.

"We cannot stay here," Lily said.

"No shit?" Dale turned around on the spot. The rope hanging from the beam above stayed slack, moving with the flow of water. With no obvious way out, they were stuck.

"We should go back inside," Logan said.

They sat around the single lamp as it cast long shadows upon their faces. They shivered with a creeping cold; even in the tropics, the water sucked the heat out of their bodies.

Logan broke the silence, "If we go back the way we came, we can get back to the top deck. We can take turns keeping watch. Maybe have a signal fire ready to go if we see a ship."

"Sure…" Dale felt crushed. "Why the fuck not?"

"Shh…" Lily stood up and moved to the door. They had left it open, waiting for Alyona to return.

"Logovo zmeya," someone shouted.

"That's not Alyona," Dale whispered.

"I do hope she is okay," Logan said quietly.

"Potok zeverya!" another voice yelled.

A chorus of shouts echoed the phrase, *"Potok zeverya!"*

"Potok zeverya!"

"I wish we knew what the fuck they were screaming about," Dale said.

"They called this place the lair of the snake. Now they are chanting, feed the beast," Lily said.

"Wait, you understand Russian?" Dale stared at her, his face incredulous.

Lily regarded him calmly. "My grandparents were Russian immigrants to Australia. I haven't heard the language in decades.

It took a while, but it is coming back to me."

"Fuck me." Dale shook his head.

"It's a good thing," Logan said. "If Lily can understand what they are saying, we know how to avoid them."

"Whatever."

"I think they have gone now." Lily cocked her head, as if listening to distant whispers. "Yes, they have moved on."

Slipping out the door, Lily crossed the flooded chamber and went to the hanging rope and gave it a tug. It held fast.

With a surprising strength for a woman that Dale guessed to be pushing seventy, she scrambled up through the waterfall and out of sight.

Logan urged Dale to go next. He crossed the swirling water, the echoes of the chanting making him even more nervous about what might be coiling in the dark water below.

With his adrenaline surging, Dale started up the rope. He told himself not to look down, but he did. In the barest light of the oil lamp, a shape flickered in the water. Something as wide as a great white shark, the light shimmering off its scales. *How fucking long is that? Twenty feet? Forty?* Dale felt his strength fail in sudden terror. That monstrous fucking thing could swallow any shark that Dale had ever seen.

Where were you when sharks took Shona, you fucking cunt! Dale climbed again, despair giving way to a furious anger that burned the cold out of his bones.

Finishing his climb up the rope, Dale swung onto the floor above, steadying himself against the rushing torrent.

"Where is Logan?" Lily asked.

"Right behind me, I hope."

The rope went tight and creaked with the weight of a man.

Dale stayed back from the edge, letting Lily lean out and grab the rope.

"Oh…" Lily gasped. Dale didn't have to ask; he knew what she had seen. He just hoped that Logan would remain blissfully unaware of the terror below him.

"Climb, Logan," Lily shouted.

The rope jerked, and Dale heard Logan cry out. A monstrous snake erupted out of the waterfall, the long serpentine body reaching the ceiling and then curving down in a vicious caricature of a question mark.

Lily sprang back from the snake and the swinging rope.

"Grab Logan!" Dale screamed.

The snake swayed slightly, its tongue flicking out to taste the air. Everything about the monster was magnified, even its cold black eyes were the size of hubcaps.

Lily slipped a hand inside her summer dress and drew out a familiar knife.

Dale tried to remember where he had seen it, then it struck him: it was the dive knife from the survival kit on the raft. The one that had gone missing a few days after they were wrecked. *Lily had the knife the whole time?*

The woman grabbed the woven rope, her wiry arms straining as she pulled it within reach.

Logan appeared through the flow of water, he shook his head and shouted something that Dale couldn't quite hear.

"Wait!" Dale yelled, comprehending a moment too late what she was doing.

Lily looked down at Logan, they made eye contact and held it long enough for Dale to draw breath to yell again. Lily slashed downwards with the knife. The razor shape edge opened a long cut down the side of Logan's face. He screamed and tossed his head against the sharp agony of it.

Lily stepped back, her intense gaze moving to the giant snake.

Dale finally moved. Rushing forward, he reached for Logan. The old man's face was a mask of blood and his eyes screwed shut.

"Logan!" Dale yelled, his hand reached out to grab the old man and pull him to safety.

The snake struck. Moving with a liquid grace, it flowed through the air and curled itself around Logan. The man's back arched and he screamed as the coiled muscle of the snake tightened around him.

Dale watched, helpless to intervene as the snake coiled tighter until Logan's body cracked under the crushing pressure. In a final move, the snake opened its jaws wider than Dale could reach and impaled Logan on fangs the length of swords.

The snake retreated into the water, carrying Logan's body with it and snapping the frayed rope like a strand of cotton.

Dale staggered away from the edge. Rounding on Lily, he screamed, "You fucking crazy bitch!"

Lily turned slowly, her face calm as granite. "It was his time to go," she said.

"You could have saved him!" Dale yelled.

"It is better to have a quick death than linger in suffering." Lily stepped towards Dale, the knife firm in her grip.

"Are you completely fucking insane?"

"Stop swearing! There is no need for that kind of language!" Lily yelled, her face flushing with sudden anger.

"Fuck you, bitch!" Dale bolted against the current. He had a head start and splashed past the opening in the ceiling where they had come down through the pipe.

A glance back in the darkness didn't show Lily following him. Dale kept going, afraid to stop in case she came up on him in the dark.

CHAPTER 15

"Dale…?" Lily's voice came through the darkness.

He froze in the corridor; afraid she might hear him moving against the water.

"I enjoyed talking to you earlier, Dale. It is the weight of our circumstance. It brings people together in ways no other experience can. I know you don't understand. You are too young. Too inexperienced. Your exposure to the cruelty of life, its fragility, is minimal. Death frightens you. That is quite natural. You need to be close to death, to hold the hands of those who are passing. Once you see their transition…then you begin to understand.

"I have seen pain in all its myriad forms. In the end, those who are dying find relief in death. The terminally ill, those injured beyond repair. They often die alone. I made it my place to be with them. To be there in their final moments. To share that experience with them.

"I told each of them the story I will now tell you. The truth of it all. My confession if you will, whispered in the ears of the dying. I told you the truth earlier. My mother was stricken with polio. We did live with my grandparents until I was eight years old. I was eight before I realized that there was a terrible thing happening in that house. My grandfather had given himself to a perverse lust. He raped my mother regularly. She, bed-ridden, paralyzed and dependent on her parents for everything. She lived in hell for most of her life. I saw him assaulting her one night. It terrified me, I admit. My dearest mother, always so caring and gentle with me. Loving and kind, with that foul beast naked and thrusting himself against her as she wept and begged him to stop. What could I do? Tell my grandmother? That was my first thought, of course. Stop this terrible thing happening. But you see, she knew. My grandmother was complicit in this atrocity. She appeared beside me outside my mother's bedroom door and silently guided me away. She took me back to bed, tucked me in, and kissed me goodnight.

"Of course, I could go to no one else for help. What would happen to mother and I if we were cast out of the house? We had no friends, and I was not enrolled in school.

"I concluded of course that my mother could be saved and my grandparents could be punished. It was simple enough. I burned them in their car. Right there in the driveway, far enough away from the house that my mother would not be in danger. By the time the fire department arrived, they were cooked.

"I stayed with mother for another ten years, then she died. Of natural causes, I assure you."

Lily paused and cocked her head, listening for any sounds of movement in the darkness. She felt the close presence of all those she had helped over the years. The old and the young, the sick and the lost. All of them dying. All of them needing her to ease their passing. All them the vessels of her confession.

Dale tensed his aching muscles, his feet had already gone

numb from the water and the forced stillness.

Now that she had stopped talking, he had no idea where Lily might be. He waited a moment longer, his fear rising like the cold ocean tide. Moving his wooden feet, he almost stumbled as the pins and needles effect rippled through them. Then something tapped him on the head. Alyona hung suspended, her limbs woven into the exposed steel beams of the ceiling. As Dale stared, she unfolded like a cat and lowered her upper half to grab him by the shoulders.

With surprising strength, she lifted Dale out of the water. "Climb up here," Alyona whispered.

Dale caught hold of the nearest beam and heaved himself on to it. The cascade of water falling from his sodden clothes was hidden by the steady dripping from everything else.

Alyona flexed with the core power of an acrobat until she returned to her position parallel to the floor.

From there, she rose to a crouch, pushing a swatch of rotting carpet aside, climbing up and out of sight. Dale followed her; anything was better than staying down here with Lily somewhere in the darkness.

CHAPTER 16

"Lily is crazy. She killed Logan. Fed him to a fucking huge snake."

"*Zver,*" Alyona replied pulling up through the hole in the floor by his arm.

"Yeah, something like that."

"*Zver,* it is name of snake. The Slaves call it Beast. Like in the Bible."

"I don't really give a fuck what they call it. It fucking ate my friend," Dale snapped.

"You cry now, yes?" Alyona stood, her hands on her narrow hips, her eyes cold.

"No." Dale felt he had cried enough. He was as dry as beef jerky.

"Then stop with your fucking whining. I came back to get you. You get killed when I not here, not my problem."

"Lily, she—"

"Fuck Lily. Fuck old man. You alive."

"Sure, where is the raft? You disappeared on us."

"I had to hide raft. Slaves come. Then I come back to get whining-boy."

"Dale, my name is Dale."

"Nyt'ye mal'chik."

"What the fuck does that mean?"

"It is Russian for, I am sorry."

"Thanks. Now let's keep moving yeah?"

Alyona moved silently in the darkness, leaving Dale feeling like a lumbering animal as he hurried after her. The stripped back walls were marked with art. From the texture and color, someone had been finger-painting in their own shit.

The ghostly woman paused and checked around a corner of the corridor. She straightened, holding a shining blade of salvaged metal high and ready. Dale waited, pressing against the wall behind Alyona. He could smell them coming, the unwashed bodies of the Slaves of God. Being out here would drive anyone insane. Lesser people would have just given up and died. Dale pressed a hand against his mouth to stifle a sudden urge to giggle. *Monk must be running a tight ship.* Shona would have rolled her eyes at that and told him off for telling Dad jokes.

Alyona swung her blade upwards like a golfer teeing off. The blade ripped through the gut of the first man to reach the corner, tearing out just below his ribs and spilling a coiled mess of internal organs out on the floor.

He dropped to his knees and fell face forward without a sound. Alyona danced. Leaping easily over the collapsing body, she slashed the throat of a woman who didn't have time to scream.

"Keep up," she said.

A sound like the breeze whispering through dead trees rose around them. Dale hesitated, "What the fuck is that?" he hissed.

"Krysy. Rats." Alyona started running down the corridor as

the noise grew louder. "Fucking run!" she called over her shoulder.

They came out of the walls, pushed their way up through the ragged patches in the floor and fell like massive black raindrops from the holes in the ceiling. These rats were the size of small dogs, their teeth filed down by constant gnawing on steel and bone. Dale fled as the swarm poured over the two fallen corpses, the bodies vanishing under the squeaking deluge.

"Fuck me…"

Alyona skidded to a halt at a T-intersection, Dale collided with her and they both went down in a heap.

Snarling, Alyona pushed Dale aside and sprang to her feet. Coming towards them were at least ten of the ragged Slaves of God. Dale stood and looked both ways down the hall.

"Run?" Dale asked when Alyona stood ready to take them all on.

She hesitated as if considering her chances of killing a dozen men and women.

"Go, that way." Alyona nodded down the corridor.

Dale took off, hearing Alyona's howl of fury as she turned and ran after him.

The Slaves took delight in the chase; they whooped and snarled, cheering each other on and banging their weapons on the walls as they charged after the two runners.

The desolate remains of the tourist cabins flashed past as Dale ran. He sprang up a stairwell, spinning around on the landing and sprinting up the next flight. Alyona swung the knife she carried and blood sprayed up the wall from a gashed cheek. She didn't break her stride, staying on Dale's heels as they ran down a matching corridor on the next deck.

"*Nalevo, idite nalevo!*" Alyona yelled.

"What the fuck are you saying?" Dale screamed over his shoulder.

"Left, motherfucker! Go left!"

Dale slid on the floor, and scrambled through a wooden door on his left. Alyona came through and slammed the door behind them. She threw her weight against it and slid a bar across that locked it down.

The muffled shrieks of the Slaves sounded on the other side and they began pounding on the wood.

"Take this and climb." Alyona shoved a bundle of raft materials at Dale and indicated a hole in the ceiling. Behind them, the wooden door began to splinter under a hail of blows.

Dale pushed the bundle up into the ceiling space. Flexing his knees, he jumped and pulled himself up. Alyona threw a second bundle to him and Dale shoved it behind his back.

"Move," Alyona demanded. Dale climbed out of the way and Alyona swarmed up the wall.

"You would be world-class at Parkour, you know," Dale said.

"*Parkur?*"

"Sure. Park-ur." Dale pressed back as Alyona slid up past him. Her skin was as filthy as his, and if his nose wasn't overwhelmed by his own stink, she might even smell bad.

Alyona stood on Dale's shoulders and slammed her hands against a hatch. Dale set his feet, wincing at the stabbing pain.

"*Yob!*" SLAM. "*Tvoyu!*" SLAM "*Mat!*" The hatch gave way with a groan of its rusted hinges.

Alyona wriggled through the gap. Her hand appeared a moment later, gesturing for Dale to hand her the bundled raft parts.

He grabbed the first load and pushed it into her hand. Dale reached for the second bundle when the door to the cabin gave way. He lifted the load over his head and shoved it at the hatch. Alyona took it and vanished again.

Dale tensed to jump for the hatch. He missed on the first attempt. A scarred hand wrapped around his ankle as he tensed to try again.

"Get the fuck off me!" Dale kicked at the head coming up through the hole and fell backwards on his ass.

The Slave clinging onto his leg came up through the hole. Dale had a moment of dread that the cannibal would sink its brown teeth into the meat of his leg. He lashed out with his other foot. The blow connected with a loud crack and the slave dropped out of sight.

Sliding backwards, Dale stood in the narrow space. He could see the leering faces of the cannibals staring up at him lit by flickering lights in the cabin below.

They started by stabbing at Dale with their spears. The metal tips sliding through the ceiling panels and making Dale move his feet in a discordant dance of panic.

"Fuckin' cunts!" he screamed at the jabbering faces. A light flared next to his head. Dale looked up as he jerked away. Alyona held a half-full glass bottle with a burning rag stuffed in the open neck.

It took him a moment to comprehend, then Dale grabbed the Molotov cocktail and threw it as hard as he could into the cabin below.

The bottle exploded, throwing burning liquid across the crowded room. Dale reached up and grabbed Alyona's hands.

She pulled him out of the smoke, the screams of the trapped and dying were the only other sign of the horror taking hold below.

Alyona crawled down a narrow tunnel, one of the claustrophobic service ducts that ran between the main decks. She stopped at a point that seemed no different to any other Dale could see. Twisting, she drew a knee up and kicked the wall out. Fresh air and the smell of the sea washed into the tight space. Coughing on the rising smoke, Dale crawled out through the gap and collapsed gasping for air on the open deck next to Alyona.

"Easy…" Dale croaked between bouts of coughing.

"Derr'mo," Alyona replied.

The night sky blazed with more stars than Dale could comprehend. "I wish Shona could see this sky."

"Shona?" Alyona sat up.

"My girlfriend. She… she didn't make it onto the ship."

"Everyone lose someone. *V'zhopu.*"

"We can get off this ship right?"

Alyona sighed and stood. "We can sail to America."

"Sure why not. I've never been to the States." Dale stood and shivered.

Alyona stared out to the dark horizon. "For Alexi."

Dale took his bearings from the stars, "For Alexi and for Shona."

"We make boat." Alyona untied the folded-up body of the raft and spread it out on the deck. Dale worked the knots on the other bundle. Inside the wrapping of a salvaged sail were the poles and cross braces that formed the frame of Alyona's boat.

"This could work…" Dale said hefting two pieces critically. "You made this yourself?"

"You not have women engineer in Australia?"

"I guess… I mean… okay."

"Men are stupid," Alyona declared.

CHAPTER 17

They worked in silence, threading the pipes together and lashing them with the plastic ties Alyona had woven into strong cords.

After an hour, they had the frame together and were finishing stretching the stitched skin of salvaged rubber sheet and sailcloth over it.

"You sure this can hold both of us?" Dale eyed the craft warily.

"*Da.* Was going to take Alexi and me. If I had found him, we would be gone before you came onboard."

"Shona always said things happen for a reason. I just wish the reasons weren't complete shit."

"Life is shit. But dying is shittier."

Dale stared at Alyona, the dehydration and terror that filled his life cracked and he grinned. "Fuckin' A. Dying is definitely shittier than living." The insanity of it burst out and he started laughing. Alyona stared at Dale, wondering if he had gone crazy. Then she started giggling, soon they both collapsed on the deck, laughing until they couldn't breathe.

Alyona recovered first. "We must move boat now. Hide it. Then I finish here and we go to America."

"You need a hand?"

"No, is easy to carry." She lifted the boat onto her shoulder and strode off down the deck until the darkness swallowed her whole.

Starting with identifying the constellations of the southern sky, Dale began counting the stars. He had reached eight hundred and twelve when a shadow blocked his view. "Hey—!" A white club of human bone crashed down, bouncing off the steel deck right where Dale's head had been a moment earlier.

He rolled away, swinging blindly with his feet and avoiding a sweeping blow. Slaves poured onto the deck, coming out of the hatchways and dropping from the higher rails. They pounded steel with their weapons, the metal blades striking sparks that flared like the stars.

"God is cruel!" Monk roared in the darkness. "He respects cruelty!"

Alyona hung from the railing of the ship, her feet scrambling to grip on the slick metal. She could hear Dale shouting and cursing the Slaves who knocked him down and carried him off. They had meat, freshly butchered from the other man. She hoped they wouldn't kill Dale tonight.

CHAPTER 18

Voices. Singing and chanting. Words in Russian.

Dale tried to tell them he didn't understand. But his throat was too dry, his tongue turned to wood behind his teeth.

I'm thirsty... He tried to wake up. Digging through silt was easier than returning to consciousness.

He heard a familiar voice. *Shona.* She called him upwards, he could hear it in her laugh. The scent of her hair. The way she studied his face when they lay close.

Water dripped on his face, moved to his mouth and broke the dried seal of his lips. Dale drank greedily, feeling life seep back into his limbs as he swallowed.

"Prosnut'sya..." Water splashed on Dale's eyes. He coughed, choking on the water pouring over him. Rolling over, Dale blinked and squinted. "Okay, I'm up."

Monk crouched, a six-foot snake curling around his neck and down his arm. "You are a message from God."

"Yeah, that's right. God says you should treat me good."

"You think you speak to God?" Monk's eyes were hidden in the dark oil of his face paint. Matted strands of hair hung over his white cheeks.

"I think you're fucking nuts."

"You would know if you spoke to God. You would know and you would be filled with his voice. His words would coil around you like the body of the serpent. You would do nothing except live the truth of those words."

"Maybe." Dale felt exhausted and angry. It was the kind of exhaustion that comes when there are no options left. When everything is fucked. The moment you stop trying to reach the surface and just let go.

"You are the message. Not the messenger." Monk dropped the empty water bottle on the floor. Dale stared at it for want of something more interesting to focus on.

"Of course you do not know what the message is. You cannot see within yourself. You are just an instrument of His will."

"You're the guy who has the hotline to God, you tell me what the message is."

"God's people need to be purified. To reach Heaven, we must survive Hell."

"It's been a while since I went to church." Dale moved to a sitting position, the smoke-stained walls of the chapel coming into focus. "I seem to remember something about God saying we are supposed to be nice to each other. Didn't Jesus die so we could all get into Heaven?"

"The gospels are a lie. Twisted and re-written to suit the minds of men who sought power here on earth."

"You're the only one who knows the truth, right?"

"It is my burden to bear."

"You're bat-shit crazy."

"All true prophets are insane in the eyes of those who do not understand the truth they bring."

"That's convenient." Dale closed his eyes. He hoped being eaten by snakes would be relatively quick and painless. If Heaven existed, he hoped that Shona would be there. He would love to see her again. Even for one last hug.

"Prosnut'sya…" Monk said again.

Dale slowly shook his head. "No speaky-da-Ruskie."

"I say, wake up."

"I am awake. I'm just tired of your bullshit."

Monk hit Dale hard enough to send him tumbling across the floor.

"You cannot deny God."

Dale groaned, gingerly probing his throbbing jaw.

"Polozhit' yego obratno v kletku," Monk gave orders to unseen followers.

Rough hands grabbed Dale and dragged him through the water. He struggled and fought, "No! No! No!" They ignored him, dumping the cursing Australian in the familiar cage. This time, a guard remained in the room to watch him.

CHAPTER 19

Huk!

Dale stirred; the guard hadn't said a word since they threw him in here. The man now lay slumped against the wall, a smear of blood marked where he had stood.

"Alyona?" Dale whispered. Rising to a crouch, he peered into the gloom.

"Dale…"

It took him a moment to recognize Lily's voice. "Lily?" For the first time, he hoped the cage was securely locked.

"Yes, Dale. How are you feeling?" The retired nurse leaned into the light, her face masked with blood and grease.

"Jesus… Lily, did you go fucking native or what?"

"It is easier to pass among them if you look like one of them." She smiled.

"You're as crazy as Monk is."

"I don't believe in God," Lily replied. "Would you like me to get you out of this cage?"

Dale stood, stretching his stiff legs and working the blood back into his limbs. "Then what?"

"Alyona, she has a boat? A raft? I want you to show me where it is."

"How the hell would I know?"

"You were with her. Monk's followers captured you and she disappeared."

"Yeah, but we didn't have a boat."

"Where's the boat, Dale?"

"I don't fucking know."

"Dale. I have told you that foul language will not be tolerated. I can walk away, leave you to your fate if you prefer. As much as it would pain me. If you do not moderate your language, I shall have no choice."

"Fine. Get me the fu—get me out of here."

"See, that wasn't so hard, now was it?" Lily smiled.

Dale forced himself to smile back.

"I have been watching since you ran away," Lily said.

"Watching?" Dale found the idea of Lily doing anything without his knowledge disturbing.

"Monk's people are maggots crawling through the decaying corpse of this ship. They are blind and barely aware of the metamorphosis they have been promised."

"No sh—I mean, no kidding?"

Lily nodded, lost in her own thoughts. "The truth of the *Mikhail Lazarov*, this ship, is darker. The hold is packed with chemical drums. Russian-made, dangerous materials. Many rusted and leaking now. That is why the crew deserted the ship; they did not have a problem with smuggling people. But carrying toxic waste? That was more than they were prepared to do."

"How do you know? Did you find someone who told you all this?"

"I found a letter, written by one of the crew. A confession."

"Confessions are your thing," Dale said.

"There are decks teeming with rats. Millions of them. They are eating each other, and anything else they can find."

"I saw them," Dale replied.

"The sea-snakes, born, swimming, living, and dying in a toxic soup of God-knows-what. I am sure a biologist would have a field day studying the specimens."

"David Attenborough would shit himself," Dale agreed.

"Do you want me to leave you in there?" Lily warned.

"No."

"There's a price of course."

"Yeah?"

"I release you from the cage, you take me to the raft."

Dale stretched; it gave him a moment to think about what he said next. "If I can find it. I don't know exactly where Alyona took it."

"It's still on the ship somewhere. Together, we will find it."

"Deal."

Lily came forward and unbolted the cage. Dale stepped out but couldn't shake the feeling he was safer inside.

CHAPTER 20

"Everyone is asleep. I always liked this time on the wards. The gentle breath of peaceful rest. The hum of machines. I would stand watch. A guardian of the dying."

Dale looked up. The hole in the ceiling had been covered with scrap metal and nailed shut. "Great, you have a way out of here?"

"Follow me." Lily glided through the curtain. The floor of the chapel was awash with water. In the dim light of the scattered lamps, snakes moved restlessly in the shallows.

"Mind your step," Lily breathed. She moved gracefully, treading with light steps through the water, the snakes undisturbed by her passing.

Dale walked carefully, staring hard at the moving flood. It was like watching a pot of boiling spaghetti, except each noodle was six feet long and deadly.

A snake swept across Dale's feet; he froze as the sinuous form curled around his calf and slipped away into the darkness.

"They flood the chapel at night and release the snakes," Lily's voice floated to him in the dim light.

"Christ…" Dale started moving again. He reached the door where Lily waited. The corridor at her back was silent and cloaked in darkness.

"We need to get outside," Dale whispered.

"The stairs are at the end of the hall. We go up two decks, and we can get out there."

"Easy," Dale muttered.

"Can you make it in the dark?"

"Not like we have any choice."

Lily went first; Dale had no intention of turning his back on her, ever. He counted to three and went after her.

The stairs were stripped like everything else, what remained felt more like the bones of a skeleton, bare metal, cold and dead in the dark under Dale's searching hands.

Lily seemed to have no issue with the pitch black. Dale could hear the slight creak of her steps on the stairs. He focused on the sound and kept moving.

He had reached the landing when Lily's voice whispered close and startling, "There's someone asleep up ahead."

The sound of someone else breathing was barely audible. Dale felt more than heard Lily moving up the stairs. He definitely heard the sound of her stabbing the sleeping person and the stifled grunt of their reaction.

She didn't come back, so Dale crept up the stairs. He could hear a sliding sound; Lily straining to drag a body?

"What are you doing?" he whispered.

"Grab her feet, we need to move the body."

Her? Dale felt around until he touched the cooling skin of the corpse. He moved his hands to the ankles, and lifted. Lily took the weight at the other end; together, they lifted the dead woman and shuffled down the corridor.

"Here." Lily stopped and set her load down.

"What?" Dale whispered, the dead woman's feet pressing against his thighs.

He heard the sound of a metal grate being dragged open. "Put her in here," Lily whispered.

They positioned the body, head and shoulders first into the hole. With some effort, they worked the rest of the body into the space behind the wall. After a moment, gravity took over, and she dropped with a cracking thud.

The familiar whispering of swarming rats rose and Dale backed away. Lily replaced the grille and wiped her hands on her sundress.

"The rats will take care of it."

"Like the giant snake took care of Logan?"

Dale could feel Lily staring at him in the dark. "You're not still mad at me about that are you, Dale?"

Biting back a scream, Dale forced his voice to sound calm. "I understand. You did what you had to. What was right."

He could smell her now, the fresh blood as she stepped right up to him, his eyes darting about in useless desperation.

"What was right…" Lily said in Dale's ear. A moment later, she moved away.

"You coming?" Lily said, closer to the stairs.

The sky had the dark stone color that heralded the coming dawn. Dale could see Lily in the star light, silhouetted in swathes of blood.

"Which way, Dale?"

Dale glanced at the sky, orienting himself against the constellations. "That way," he pointed. "We were putting the raft together, that way."

CHAPTER 21

Alyona listened to the rats rising in a dark tide through the walls. Monk had always been careful, keeping the vermin caged or trapped in parts of the ship where they couldn't overwhelm his people. Someone had let them out. Probably those stupid outsiders, the ones who found Alexi's body. Little Alexi, his head full of dreams of America. Knowing that he was dead brought some relief, a sense of closure. The nightmare was over for Alexi, at least.

If the rats were loose, they were unstoppable. You might fight off the Slaves of God, even the monstrous snakes. If the rats got you, you were fucked. Alyona had seen people kill themselves rather than let the rats take them.

The rats whispered, telling her she had run out of time. The Australian was either dead, or on his own. She had to leave now. Take her memories and Alexi's bag and get off the ship.

Remember the plan! Yes, the promise she had made to Alexi, to herself, and to God.

The drums in the dry sections of the ship stood in densely packed rows. They had been in wooden crates originally, but now the wood was gone. She took a heavy blade and slammed it into the side of the nearest steel drum. Thick, viscous liquid gushed out, spilling on the floor and spreading.

Alyona moved on, finding the other rooms with their stacks of drums. She cracked one in each room, until the acrid fumes threatened to choke her.

She only had one Molotov cocktail left. Using her spare to save the Australian had been a mistake. She could only hope one would be enough.

Leaving doors open, she moved through the ship. The rats were stirring and it would be light soon. She hurried on.

"Is the meat still fresh?"

"Yeah. We took his other leg. But he's still alive."

Alyona froze. Slaves of God were coming down the stairs. She ducked into an abandoned cabin and pressed herself against the wall.

"What about the others?"

"The boy is in the cage. The young bitch, Monk offered her to God. She was not worthy."

"I would have fucked her first."

"You would fuck anything."

"Do you think we will get to Heaven, before we're all gone?"

"Monk says it will be soon. The new ones, they are a sign."

"I pray it is soon. I don't want to be chosen."

"We find these new ones and none of us will be chosen for a while."

Alyona held her breath as the two cannibals passed the cabin. So Dale was back in the cage. She would have to move fast if she wanted to get him out. *Why bother? What use is he? He bought Alexi back to me.* That stopped her breath. The bag she now carried, Alexi had clung to it always. Hiding it when the others were around, always reading from it, running his fingers over the pictures and murmuring the names of the Statue of Liberty, the Disneyland, and the Yankee Stadium.

For Alexi. Another thought struck her, what if Dale had told Monk about the boat? What if they already knew and were looking for it? *Have faith.* Alexi would have prayed. Not to the dark god that Monk spoke to, but to the God of their mother's faith, the one who forgave all sins and demanded no sacrifice.

The chapel and the cage would be opened soon. The Slaves would gather for Monk's dawn sermon, and afterwards, they would feast. The thought of food made Alyona's stomach rumble.

Alexi had been the one to find the secret ways through the ship. He avoided the followers of Monk who did things to the young ones that Alyona knew all too well.

Climbing into one of the service ducts, she went up one deck, then down toward the stern of the ship. Traversing an empty corridor, she crept into the duct that would lead her to the anteroom of the chapel. The opening had been barricaded; she peered down through the gaps and could see the cage was empty.

Derr`mo. Shit. They had already taken Dale.

Alyona worked her way back, climbing up ducts and spaces between the walls until she emerged on the open deck.

It was still dark, but the darkness was changing. Good time for fishing.

They had fished at first, but catching anything had been challenging. Catching enough fish for everyone had proved impossible. Fights broke out and the first deaths were over the few morsels of fish.

Monk had taken control and enforced order. At first, no one asked where he got the meat from. It was enough to eat and live.

When God started talking through him, the others seized the

hope he offered. Madness and death were all that remained now. The hope of rescue or landfall had faded in time, and now they were bound to Monk and his dark testament.

"We were putting the raft together, that way." Dale's voice.

Alyona crouched and peered through the railing. On the lower deck, she could see the shadowy figures of Dale and the old woman, Lily. Dale followed her along the deck and they stopped where the raft was put together.

"Alyona took it somewhere. I have no idea where she went," Dale said.

"How big is this raft?"

"It's about the size of a dinghy. Alyona had made a frame of aluminum tubes and a hull out of salvaged plastic and rubber sheet. I reckon it will float. She even has a sail rigged up and ready to go. Could get some good mileage out of it."

Alyona frowned; was Dale going to steal her boat and sail off with the old woman?

Drawing her knife, Alyona moved along the railing, keeping pace with the two below.

"It'll be light soon," Dale said. "We should find Alyona. It's her boat. She's the one who says—"

"Says what, Dale? Who goes on her boat and who doesn't? There wouldn't be room for three of us, would there? Staying here is a death sentence. You and I both know that."

"We have no right to take the boat without her."

"Of course we do. Survival gives us that right. You get nothing in this world if you don't take it."

"Regardless of who gets hurt?" Dale stepped over the crushed skull fragments of a person.

"Someone always gets hurt. Life is much simpler when you

accept that."

"Easy for you to say. You kill people for laughs."

"I have never killed anyone. I have helped people."

"You sure as shit didn't help Logan."

"I did help him. Logan could never survive. It was easier for him this way."

"You could have killed yourself. Made it easier for everyone."

"I can survive. It is what I have always done. I have my doubts about you though, Dale."

With a sickening certainty, Dale realized that Lily was never going to let him on the boat.

"What is that?" Lily asked. She pointed at a sun-bleached plastic fuel container that hung from the rail on a strap of plastic rope tied through the molded handle.

Alyona dropped from above, landing like a cat behind Lily and sending the older woman sprawling.

"It is part of the plan," Alyona said.

"Shit!" Dale yelped.

"We must leave ship now," Alyona lashed out with a foot and kicked Lily across the head. The woman slumped to the deck and lay still.

"The boat is okay?" Dale asked.

"Of course. Russian-made boat. Best in world."

"Of course." Dale nodded.

Alyona started twisting the cap off the plastic fuel container. "Vodka. I make."

"Maybe we should get off the ship before we celebrate?"

"Not for drinking. For burning."

Alyona tipped the container and splashed the clear liquid

across the deck. Digging in the leather satchel, she stuffed a cloth wick into the neck of a glass bottle.

"Molotov cocktail," Dale said.

"Da."

"Dale…" Lily called. She rose to her feet, swaying slightly.

"Shit."

"Dale, we are survivors, you and I. We need to fulfill that destiny."

"Whatever you are going to do, you had better hurry up," Dale warned.

Alyona started striking a spark along the edge of her blade. "Do you have match or Zippo?"

"No?"

"So shut fuck up."

"It doesn't have to be like this Dale." Lily was coming towards them, stumbling slightly, a trickle of fresh blood running down from her hairline and across her nose.

A light flared, the wick of the Molotov cocktail bursting into flame.

"Go to front of ship. Get on boat," Alyona ordered.

Dale backed away, wondering what Alyona was waiting for.

Lily stepped into the spreading pool of spilled alcohol, and Alyona threw the burning bottle as hard as she could. The air turned white in a flash of fire.

Lily screamed as the fire exploded around her. Dale ran for the bow, Alyona keeping pace with him.

"Is she dead?" Dale panted.

"I did not stop to ask."

The bow of the *Mikhail Lazarov* was crusted in salt and rust. Alyona's footprints were the only recent marks.

Alyona gestured to the rail. "You go down rope, boat is down there."

The fire continued to rage, liquid fire flowing through gaps in the deck and falling in steady drops of blazing rain.

The rising fumes of the breached drums met the burning fuel. The entire ship shuddered as a fireball ripped through the lower decks. Rusted steel disintegrated in a storm of shrapnel, tearing through the barricades and incinerating anyone caught in its path.

Monk shouted orders and his people ran for the deck. The water on the floor of the chapel began to warm as the inferno raged beneath it. Monk nodded, a smile creasing the grime-filled lines of his face. The time had come.

CHAPTER 22

"Reckon we can jump?" Dale peered into the shadow cast by the ship. Alyona's boat was somewhere down there, in the dark.

Alyona looked at Dale as if he was an idiot. "You want to die? You jump. I make rope for ladder. We climb down." The ladder turned out to be a rope with large knots at regular intervals. Alyona tied it to the railing and tossed the end into the dark.

The ship groaned deep in its steel belly as another explosion ripped through the interior. On the port side, a hull section tore open, allowing seawater to rush in, and the ship began to list.

Scrambling out onto the deck, the Slaves of God blinked at the acrid smoke burning their eyes. "Hell! Hell is upon us! Monk save us!" they cried.

Monk joined them on the deck. "The time has come! God has heard the cries of our suffering! Our salvation is at hand!"

"Strike down the unbelievers! Destroy the outsiders! Then we shall be free!"

His followers howled in a frenzy of righteous terror and charged along the deck at his command. The fire blazed through cracks in the deck, searing skin and hair as they ran through the geysers of flame.

Rats fled for the deck as their world was devoured in the apocalyptic inferno. A river of squirming bodies clogged the corridors and hatchways. The shrill squeaking was audible over the lower pitched howl of the fire-storm.

A swarm of vermin poured onto the deck, maddened by the smoke and flames. They fell on the charging cannibals and tore them to pieces. Monk's people howled and fought, lashing out at the giant rats and tossing the creatures over the rail.

In the lower decks, the millions of sea snakes that had bred, mutated, and thrived in the toxic waters of the flooded hold, followed the new currents and spilled out into the open sea. Like the rats, they formed a living carpet of squirming monsters.

The ship slid further to one side as the water poured in and more of the decaying infrastructure gave way.

Dale clung to the rail at the bow of the ship, the deck underfoot tilting at a crazy angle.

"Get down the rope!" Alyona yelled. Dale nodded, mute with terror.

Rats stampeded through the flames, blazing fur and singing flesh adding to the stink in the air. Dale scrambled over the rail and gripped the rope. Going hand over hand, he lowered himself until he felt the rubber sides of the boat bobbing on the gentle swell.

"Alyona! Come on!"

Alyona glanced down; Dale had made it. He was safe. The fire would cleanse all the sin. All the evil. It would be as close to justice as Alexi's killers would ever come.

Monk, she would kill herself.

With a casual sweep of the jagged blade, Alyona slashed the

rope, letting it drop in a loose coil in the boat below. She walked towards the fire without looking back.

The first of the Slaves of God came through the flames, singed and smoking, eyes reddened and wide with terror as they ran at Alyona. She swung her blade, gutting a man and sending his guts sliding across the deck.

A second man ran at her, his howls of fury turning to screams as the roaring fire engulfed him. Alyona brought her weapon down and buried it in the screaming man's shoulder. He barely seemed to notice the new injury as she twisted and jerked the blade free. The man tumbled to the deck and lay still.

Fire jetted through open hatches and doorways, channeling the flames into blowtorch intensity. Each explosion tore a new hole, and the blast sent more of the Slaves tumbling over the side and into the water below.

She saw glimpses of Monk as he urged his people forward, shouting that God would protect them from the flames. If they proved their faith, they would be saved.

Thick black smoke blinded Alyona, hiding her enemies and threatening to choke her. Slinging the weapon onto her shoulder, she climbed the rail. Hanging by her hands, she moved towards the stern of the ship, wincing at the heat searing her knuckles.

The screams of the burning men and women merged with the roar of the flames. A fresh wave of escaping rats poured over the rail. Alyona struggled to keep her grip as they crashed down on her head and shoulders. Alyona's vision filled with flashing teeth and the horror of burnt vermin.

Throwing her body against the metal wall of the hull, Alyona knocked the animals that still clung to her into the water below. She hissed as the skin of her arms scraped the rusting steel, leaving her red and stinging.

With the last of her strength, Alyona pulled herself up and climbed back onto the deck, the fire raging behind her. Monk straightened up as he saw her striding towards him.

"Alyona…?"

"I have come to kill you, Monk."

"What makes you think you can kill me?"

"Alexi. Two years of enduring your madness. The lies you told me."

"Alexi?" Monk looked confused for a moment.

"My brother. You gave him to your people. They hurt him. He learned to hide. He got really good at hiding. Until even I couldn't find him."

"Children are the first to be taken to God."

"But you will never see Him." Alyona lifted her blade and charged.

Monk stood unmoving until she swung at him. He ducked and Alyona's sword struck the deck. Monk lashed out with his foot, his sweep knocking Alyona off her feet.

She rolled and sprang up, swinging and jabbing with the heavy blade. Monk hefted the bone club he carried and parried her blows.

"Your faith gives you strength, Alyona. I could have made life so sweet for you. Instead, you refuse everything I offered. You brought great suffering down upon yourself and your brother during the time of our exodus."

"Ebis' konyom," Alyona snarled.

"I forgive you," Monk replied. "You will go to God, with my blessing."

"You will go to Hell!" Alyona attacked, smashing at Monk

with the heavy blade. He knocked her blade aside with the bone club. He swung at her head and she blocked with the sword. The strike jarred her hands. Monk struck again, sending Alyona's sword skittering across the deck. She dived after it. Monk's club smashed down where she had stood a moment before.

Alyona crashed against a steel door and stumbled to her feet. Dark smoke swirled on the other side of the thick porthole. The fire behind the door had reduced to a smoldering glow in the oxygen-starved room. Turning, she pressed her back against the metal, feeling the heat rising against her skin.

Monk kicked her sword aside, and rested the shaft of his bone club on his shoulder. "It ends now, Alyona. I deliver your body to God. Your soul will be judged."

Monk took a baseball batter's grip on his club. He twisted, ready to swing. Alyona leaned down on the latch of the steel door and heaved the door open with all her strength.

Shielded by the door, she felt the inrush of air and the clang of Monk's club smashing into the steel. The hot cloud of explosive gases took a deep gulp of oxygen and exploded in a fireball that burned the screaming flesh from Monk's body. He catapulted backwards, striking the rail and shattering his spine.

Alyona kicked the door shut and snatched up the sword. Monk was dead, his skin blackened and crisp. She took his head anyway because delivering the final blow gave her satisfaction.

CHAPTER 23

When the rope tumbled down around him, Dale started yelling for Alyona. He couldn't see her at the rail, and with the rope cut, he had no way of getting back up there to find out what had happened to her.

He waited for her, listening to the screams of the dying and the roar of the spreading fire. The eastern sky was hidden in a fog bank of black smoke. Whatever the ship was carrying, it burned really well.

Amid the debris field of scorched bodies, charcoal lumps, and flotsam drifting around the boat, something else disturbed the water. The snakes pouring out of the flooded holds were moving in a living river. They coiled and squirmed in a thick mat scraping under the rubber hull of the small boat.

"Fuck me..." Dale muttered. There were snakes as far as he could see in the flickering light of the inferno.

Holding one of the paddles Alyona had made, Dale stood ready to smack the shit out of anything that dared stick its forked tongue above the surface.

The seething highway of snakes rocked the boat, following a reptilian instinct to move away from the stricken ship. Dale dipped his paddle into clear water and moved the boat away from the ship. The bow lifted, sending waves surging that forced Dale to paddle harder. The ship was sinking now, rolling onto its side and beginning the long descent to the distant seabed.

"Alyona!" Dale screamed through the clouds of smoke and steam. After all she had done to save him, she didn't deserve to die on the ship.

"Dale!" Alyona appeared at the rail, her body stained black with soot and grease.

"I have to jump!" she yelled.

"You wanna die? You jump!" he yelled back, laughing with the relief of seeing her again.

She climbed out onto the tilted side of the hull. With her arms outstretched for balance, Alyona ran down the rolling curve and leapt. Two seconds later, she plunged, feet first into the water and disappeared in a boiling patch of foam.

Dale scanned the water, paddling desperately towards the point where Alyona had gone under. Snakes still flowed past, though in far less numbers than before. She surfaced and treaded water, waving to Dale when he shouted. Paddling faster, he drew up alongside.

"Take my hand," Dale instructed. Leaning out, he jerked his hand back as a striped shape rose from below. Pushing a bow wave ahead of it, the giant snake called The Beast, exploded out of the water, it's hissing maw snapping shut on empty air.

"Fuck!" Dale yelled. He had no weapons, just two makeshift paddles and a patched sail.

The giant snake would tear through the tiny boat like it was made of wet Kleenex.

"Get out of here!" Alyona yelled. She doubled over and dived out of sight. Dale put his paddle to the water, arms straining as he tried to put as much distance between himself and the monster as possible.

The boat tipped to one side, almost throwing Dale into the sea. He looked around, afraid that the snake was coming onboard. A badly burned arm with raw flesh glistening and oozing fluid draped over the side. Alyona didn't look burned when she jumped off the ship. Dale dropped the paddle and scrambled over to help.

The remains of Lily's face appeared over the side; her skin had melted, and patches of blackened tissue hung from her bare scalp like strips of peeling paint.

Her teeth bared, Lily slashed at Dale with the dive knife. He fell back, feeling the blade slice through his T-shirt, his skin, and scrape against his ribs.

The boat rose on the swell of an enormous mass passing underneath it. Lily rose into the air, her fire-ravaged body jerking helplessly. The Beast clamped down tighter with fangs the size of fence palings. Lily stared at Dale and he couldn't hear what she was trying to say. The Beast sank beneath the waves, dragging her out of sight.

Alyona surfaced and gasped for air right behind Dale. He twisted around and grabbed her arm, heaving her out of the water and into the bottom of the rubber-hulled boat.

They lay there panting, letting the boat drift on the swirling currents and waves in the wake of the sinking of the *Mikhail Lazarov*.

CHAPTER 24

"Monakh mertv," Alyona whispered. *"Monakh mertv."*

"My thoughts exactly," Dale replied, wincing at the searing pain in his side where the salt water was seeping into his knife wound.

"Idiot," Alyona muttered. "You should have run away with boat, like scared boy."

"No good being the captain of a vessel, if you don't have any crew to give orders to," Dale replied.

"When I reach America, I will never go on boat again."

Dale didn't doubt it. It would be a long time before he wanted to sail again.

Alyona sat up. "We must raise sail, and paddle. There is little water, but no food."

"Hey, I'm the captain," Dale said, with a pained grin.

"Idiot," she said again and smiled at him.

Alyona paddled until they were clear of the drifting fog of smoke and steam left in the wake of the derelict ship.

Looking back, they couldn't see any sign of the *Mikhail Lazarov*, just a pool of burning liquid on the surface marked the spot where she had gone down.

*

Dale sat cross-legged on the floor of the boat, keeping pressure on his knife wound and trying to focus on the horizon. Without a rudder, keeping a steady course was almost impossible. The lack of surface features meant he could only navigate by the passage of the sun. When night fell eventually, he could steer them by the stars.

His stomach gurgled, empty and complaining. He hadn't eaten anything in at least twenty-four hours. The shade provided by Alyona's sail protected them from the worst of the tropical sun, and he was counting the minutes until they could have more of their remaining water supplies.

"We still sail west?" Alyona asked from the back of the boat. She held a paddle over the stern, using it as a rudder while the wind filled their sail.

"Yeah..." Dale closed his eyes and tried not to think about food, or water, or painkillers. "You brought water, but no food?"

"I did not have time for find food."

"Not even a fishing line..."

Alyona knelt behind Dale; the boat was small enough that she could reach out and touch him from anywhere in the tiny craft. Her own body cried out for food too. She tried to remain focused, to remind herself that Dale was a friend. Survival on the ship had meant doing unspeakable things. Killing others and eating their flesh. When faced with the choice of eat or die, Alyona had chosen to live. Staring at the back of Dale's head, she felt her stomach clench with hunger and her mouth flood with saliva.

Her grip tightened on the shaft of the paddle. A blow to the side of the head would stun him. She could keep Dale alive for a few days, bound with wire and disabled. It would be the best way to keep the meat fresh for longer.

Drawing breath, Alyona made ready to strike. Dale jerked and then rose up on his knees, shading his eyes against the glare.

"A ship!" he yelled. "A ship!"

Alyona wondered if he was imagining it, a mirage caused by dehydration and blood loss. She adjusted her position, staring out to the horizon and trying to follow where Dale pointed.

There! A ship coming towards them, cutting through the Pacific swell with the grace and ease of a vessel under full power.

*

Duty officer Naota Mitsuro focused on the console in front of him. The sky through the wide Perspex windshield of the Japanese freighter, *Sapporo Sunrise,* was clear and filled with the perfect light of early afternoon.

Next to him, Captain Takahiro Fujiwara scanned the way ahead with a large pair of binoculars. The fire on the horizon had been spotted just before dawn, though no distress signal had been detected. It was said that Fujiwara could navigate a ship without instruments and in complete darkness. None of his crew doubted his confidence in finding the source of the fire and smoke even after it had faded from the morning sky.

*

A Zodiac craft zipped across the light swell, the two people rescued from the primitive boat sat on the floor of the inflatable.

One male, one female, in their early twenties, by the medic's estimation. Both were suffering dehydration and malnutrition. The male also had a shallow knife wound across his chest. The medical officer had tended to it when they were taken off their boat.

Gaijin, the radio report said. The man was Australian, the woman was Russian. Neither had said anything that made any sense about how they came to be out here in the middle of the South Pacific in a boat made of salvaged scraps.

Mitsuro stood at the rail, the *Sapporo Sunrise* barely rocking under his feet as they waited for the outboard to complete the rescue mission. The crew lowered the cables and began to winch the Zodiac back on board.

The crew stepped off and eagerly helped the two strangers onto the deck.

Stepping in front of the two guests, Mitsuro saluted and addressed them in English, "I am Officer Naoto Mitsuro. I welcome you on behalf of Captain Takahiro Fujiwara onboard the *Sapporo Sunrise.*"

The man nodded. Smiling through cracked lips, he tried to bow, in a commendable show of respect, but the effort caused him to collapse in a faint.

"Take them to medical bay," Medical Officer Akiro ordered.

"Are they sick?" Mitsuro asked.

"No, Officer Mitsuro. As I reported to the captain, they are dehydrated, malnourished, and the man has a fresh knife wound."

Mitsuro nodded; contagious illness could be dangerous on the closed environment of a ship.

The *Gaijin* woman regarded everyone with a calm expression. No one on board spoke Russian, and she hadn't indicated she understood Japanese or English.

"See to it they are given water and food," Mitsuro ordered.

Alyona allowed the crew to take them below decks and drank the water they offered. They put Dale in a sick bay and treated his wound, giving him IV fluids.

A smiling cook presented her with *Miso* soup. She tasted a spoonful and couldn't stomach any more. Her body craved something else and she could wait until the time was right. With the fully crewed ship, there would be more than enough for her to eat.

The End

CHECK OUT OTHER GREAT
DEEP SEA THRILLERS

MEGA
by Jake Bible

There is something in the deep. Something large. Something hungry. Something prehistoric.
And Team Grendel must find it, fight it, and kill it.
Kinsey Thorne, the first female US Navy SEAL candidate has hit rock bottom. Having washed out of the Navy, she turned to every drink and drug she could get her hands on. Until her father and cousins, all ex-Navy SEALS themselves, offer her a way back into the life: as part of a private, elite combat Team being put together to find and hunt down an impossible monster in the Indian Ocean. Kinsey has a second chance, but can she live through it?

THE BLACK
by Paul E Cooley

Under 30,000 feet of water, the exploration rig Leaguer has discovered an oil field larger than Saudi Arabia, with oil so sweet and pure, nations would go to war for the rights to it. But as the team starts drilling exploration well after exploration well in their race to claim the sweet crude, a deep rumbling beneath the ocean floor shakes them all to their core. Something has been living in the oil and it's about to give birth to the greatest threat humanity has ever seen.

"The Black" is a techno/horror-thriller that puts the horror and action of movies such as Leviathan and The Thing right into readers' hands. Ocean exploration will never be the same."

CHECK OUT OTHER GREAT
DEEP SEA THRILLERS

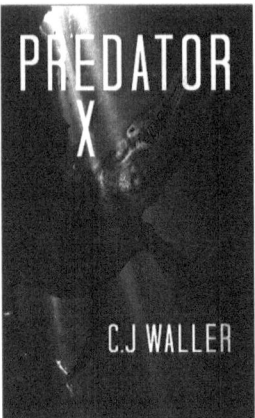

PREDATOR X
by C.J Waller

When deep level oil fracking uncovers a vast subterranean sea, a crack team of cavers and scientists are sent down to investigate. Upon their arrival, they disappear without a trace. A second team, including sedimentologist Dr Megan Stoker, are ordered to seek out Alpha Team and report back their findings. But Alpha team are nowhere to be found – instead, they are faced with something unexpected in the depths. Something ancient. Something huge. Something dangerous. Predator X

DEAD BAIT
by Tim Curran

A husband hell-bent on revenge hunts a Wereshark...A Russian mail order bride with a fishy secret...Crabs with a collective consciousness...A vampire who transforms into a Candiru...Zombie piranha...Bait that will have you crawling out of your skin and more. Drawing on horror, humor with a helping of dark fantasy and a touch of deviance, these 19 contemporary stories pay homage to the monsters that lurk in the murky waters of our imaginations. If you thought it was safe to go back in the water...Think Again!

CHECK OUT OTHER GREAT
DEEP SEA THRILLERS

LAMPREYS
by Alan Spencer

A secret government tactical team is sent to perform a clean sweep of a private research installation. Horrible atrocities lurk within the abandoned corridors. Mutated sea creatures with insane killing abilities are waiting to suck the blood and meat from their prey.

Unemployed college professor Conrad Garfield is forced to assist and is soon separated from the team. Alone and afraid, Conrad must use his wits to battle mutated lampreys, infected scientists and go head-to-head with the biggest monstrosity of all.

Can Conrad survive, or will the deadly monsters suck the very life from his body?

DEEP DEVOTION
by M.C. Norris

Rising from the depths, a mind-bending monster unleashes a wave of terror across the American heartland. Kate Browning, a Kansas City EMT confronts her paralyzing fear of water when she traces the source of a deadly parasitic affliction to the Gulf of Mexico. Cooperating with a marine biologist, she travels to Florida in an effort to save the life of one very special patient, but the source of the epidemic happens to be the nest of a terrifying monster, one that last rose from the depths to annihilate the lost continent of Atlantis.

Leviathan, destroyer, devoted lifemate and parent, the abomination is not going to take the extermination of its brood well.

CHECK OUT OTHER GREAT DEEP SEA THRILLERS

THEY RISE
by **Hunter Shea**

Some call them ghost sharks, the oldest and strangest looking creatures in the sea.

Marine biologist Brad Whitley has studied chimaera fish all his life. He thought he knew everything about them. He was wrong. Warming ocean temperatures free legions of prehistoric chimaera fish from their methane ice suspended animation. Now, in a corner of the Bermuda Triangle, the ocean waters run red. The 400 million year old massive killing machines know no mercy, destroying everything in their path. It will take Whitley, his climatologist ex-wife and the entire US Navy to stop them in the bloodiest battle ever seen on the high seas.

SERPENTINE
by **Barry Napier**

Clarkton Lake is a picturesque vacation spot located in rural Virginia, great for fishing, skiing, and wasting summer days away.

But this summer, something is different. When butchered bodies are discovered in the water and along the muddy banks of Clarkton Lake, what starts out as a typical summer on the lake quickly turns into a nightmare.

This summer, something new lives in the lake...something that was born in the darkest depths of the ocean and accidentally brought to these typically peaceful waters.

It's getting bigger, it's getting smarter...and it's always hungry.

www.ingramcontent.com/pod-product-compliance
Lightning Source LLC
Chambersburg PA
CBHW052000170626
46808CB00007B/2706